D0984520

BY THE SAME AUTHOR

Contents

A to B

There it was again, like a signal along a wire. A clear brilliant flash of pain from *A* to *B*. What was *A*? What was *B*? Kleinzeit didn't want to know. His hypotenuse was on that side, he thought. Maybe not. He'd always been afraid to look at anatomical diagrams. Muscles, yes. Organs, no. Nothing but trouble to be expected from organs.

Flash. *A* to *B* again. His diapason felt hard and swollen. His scalp was dry and flaky. He put his face in front of the bathroom mirror.

I exist, said the mirror.

What about me? said Kleinzeit.

Not my problem, said the mirror.

Ha ha, laughed the hospital bed. It was nowhere near Kleinzeit, hadn't ever seen him, was in another part of town altogether. Ha ha, laughed the hospital bed, and sang a little song that hummed through its iron limbs and chipped enamel. You and me, *A* to *B*. I have a pillow for you at my head, said the bed, I have a chart for you at my foot. Sister and her nurses listen through the night. Drip-feed tubes and bottles, oxygen cylinders and masks. Everything laid on. Don't be a stranger.

Push off, said Kleinzeit. He left the mirror empty and went to his job, staying behind his face through the corridors of the Underground and into a train. Attaché case in hand, Thucydides under his arm, the Penguin edition of *The Peloponnesian War*. His carrying book, he hadn't begun to read it yet.

NOTHING HAPPENED, said the headline on the tabloid next to him. He ignored it, looked at the naked girl on the next page, then screwed his head round to see the headline again. NOTHING HAPPENED AGAIN, said the headline. Do you mind? said the face that was reading the paper. It turned away with the headline and the naked girl. Brute, thought Kleinzeit, and closed his eyes.

What is there to tell you? he said to an unknown audience in his mind. What's the difference who I am or if I am?

The audience shifted in their seats, yawned.

All right, said Kleinzeit, let me put it this way: you read a book, and in the book there's this man sitting in his room all alone. Right?

The audience nodded.

Right, said Kleinzeit. But he isn't really alone, you see. The writer is there to tell about it, you're there to read about it. He's not alone the way I'm alone. You're not alone when there's somebody there to see it and tell about it. Me, I'm alone.

What else is new? said the audience.

Possibility of nothing this evening, clearing towards morning, said a weather report.

Let me put it this way, said Kleinzeit. This will bring us down to fundamentals: I have a Gillette Techmatic razor. The blade is a continuous band of steel, and after every five shaves I wind it to the next number. Number one is the last, which is of course significant, yes? Then I stay on number one for ten, fifteen shaves maybe, before I get a new cartridge. I ask myself why. There you have it, eh?

The audience had left, the empty seats yawned at him.

Kleinzeit got out of the train, poured into the morning rush in the corridor. Among the feet he saw a sheet of yellow paper, A4 size, on the floor, unstepped-on. He picked it up. Clean on both sides. He put it in his attaché case. He rode up on the escalator, looking up the skirt of the girl nine steps above him. Bottom of the morning, he said to himself.

Kleinzeit went up in the lift, walked into his office, sat down at his desk. He dialled Dr Pink's number and made an appointment. That's the way to do it, said the bed in the hospital on the other side of town. Sister and I will take care of everything, and you get a bottle of orange squash on your locker like everyone else.

I won't think about it now, thought Kleinzeit. He took the sheet of yellow paper from his attaché case. Thick paper it was, coarse in texture, crude and strong in its colour. It wanted a plain deal table, whitewashed walls, a bare room, thought Kleinzeit. In stories there were plain deal tables. Young men sat at them and wrote on ordinary foolscap. Their single coat hung from a single peg in the whitewashed wall. Were there plain deal tables, bare rooms? Kleinzeit put the paper into his typewriter with a sheet of carbon paper and a sheet of flimsy, shook some dandruff over the machine and began to write a television commercial for Bonzo Toothpaste.

Sister woke up, got out of bed, rose like the dawn. Rosy-fingered, rosy-toed, rosy-nippled. Tall, firm, shapely, Junoesque. Bathed and brushed her teeth. Plain white bra, Marks & Spencer knickers. Nothing fancy. Put on her uniform, her cap, her firm black Sister shoes.

Ward A4, please, she told the shoes. They took her there. What a pleasure to see her walk! The walls were cool and fresh with it on either side, the corridors smiled with reflected Sister.

In her office Sister did her office things, smoked a cigarette, unlocked the medicine locker, looked out on her empire. Men coughed and groaned, ogling her with eyes that bulged above oxygen masks. Someday my prince will come, thought Sister.

She walked among them, borne gracefully on her Sister shoes, trailing clouds of mercy and libido, followed by the medicine trolley. 'Aaahh!' they sighed. 'Ooohh!' they groaned. Deeply they breathed in oxygen, demurely peed in bottles underneath the bedclothes. Which bed will it be? thought Sister.

It was raining. The daylight in the ward was silvery, musical. The ceiling was ornately braced, like the roof of a Victorian railway station platform. Freshly painted cream-coloured Victorian knee-braces. Silver rainlight, green blankets, white sheets and pillowslips, patients in their proper places, crisp young nurses, blue and white, neatly ministering. Everything shipshape, thought Sister. Which bed will it be?

'How's it going?' said the Creative Director from between his sideburns.

'I think I've got it,' said Kleinzeit from under his dandruff. 'We open on a man pushing a barrow full of rocks. No music, just the sound of his breathing and the creaking of the barrow and the sound of the rocks bumping along. Then we move in for a close-up. Big smile as he takes a tube of Bonzo out of his pocket, holds it up, doesn't say a word. What do you think?'

The Creative Director sat down in his tight trousers, didn't light a cigarette because he didn't smoke.

Kleinzeit lit a cigarette. '*Cinema verité* approach,' he said.

'Why a barrow full of rocks?' said the Creative Director, ten years younger than Kleinzeit.

'Why not?' said Kleinzeit. He paused as the pain flashed from A to B. 'It's as good as anything else. It's better than a lot of things.'

'You're fired,' said the Creative Director in his tapered shirt.

At Dr Pink's

'The hypotenuse is a funny organ,' said Dr Pink in his Harley Street surgery. Dr Pink was fifty-five or so, every inch a gentleman, and looked as if he'd go another hundred years without even breathing hard. There were about £200 worth of magazines in the waiting room. The surgery was equipped with a tin of Band-Aids, a needle for taking blood samples, a little rack of test tubes, and an electric fire of the Regency period. Dr Pink had a stethoscope too. He examined it, flicked some earwax off it. 'We don't know an awful lot about the hypotenuse,' he said. 'Nor the diapason either, for that matter. You can go right through life without ever knowing you have either of them, or they can act up and give you no end of trouble.'

'It's probably nothing, eh?' said Kleinzeit. 'Just this little twinge from A to B ...' There it went again, this time like a red-hot iron bar jammed crosswise in him. 'This little twinge from A to B,' he said. 'Probably everybody has it now and then, I suppose, hmm?'

'No,' said Dr Pink. 'I doubt that I get three cases a year.'

Three cases of what, Kleinzeit almost asked, but didn't. 'And they're nothing serious, eh?' he said.

'How's your vision?' said Dr Pink. He opened Kleinzeit's folder, looked into it. 'Any floating spots or specks?'

'Doesn't everybody have those?' said Kleinzeit.

'What about your hearing?' said Dr Pink. 'Ever hear a sort of seething in a perfectly silent room?'

'Isn't that just the acoustics of the room?' said Kleinzeit. 'I mean, rooms *do* seethe when there's silence, don't they? Just the faintest high-pitched sibilance?'

'Your barometric pressure's good,' said Dr Pink, still

looking into the folder. 'Your barometric pressure's like that of a much younger man.'

'I go for a run every morning,' said Kleinzeit. 'Mile and a half.'

'Good,' said Dr Pink. 'We'll book you into hospital right away. Tomorrow all right for you?'

'Lovely,' said Kleinzeit. He sighed, leaned back in his chair. Then he sat up straight. 'Why do I have to go to hospital?' he said.

'Best see where we are with this,' said Dr Pink. 'Run off a few tests, that sort of thing. Nothing to worry about.'

'Right,' said Kleinzeit. That afternoon he bought a pair of adventurous-looking pyjamas, selected from his shelves books for the hospital. He packed Ortega y Gasset, *Meditations on Quixote*. He'd already read that, wouldn't have to read it again. Thucydides he would carry in his hand.

Arrival

'Ahhh!' groaned Sister as she came in Dr Krishna's arms. 'You make love like a god,' she said later when they lay side by side, smoking in the dark.

'Marry me,' said Dr Krishna. He was young and dark and beautiful and talented.

'No,' said Sister.

'Whom are you waiting for?' said Dr Krishna.

Sister shrugged.

'I've watched you walking through your ward,' said Dr Krishna. 'You're waiting for a man to turn up in one of the beds. What're you waiting for, a sick millionaire?'

'Millionaires aren't in wards,' said Sister.

'What then?' said Dr Krishna. 'What sort of man? And why a sick one? Why not a well man?'

Sister shrugged.

In the morning her firm black Sister shoes took her to Ward A4. In a bed by the window lay Kleinzeit, looking at her as if he could see through her clothes, Marks & Spencer and all.

Oh no, thought Kleinzeit when he saw Sister, this is too much. Even if I were well, which I'm probably not, even if I were young, which I no longer am, this is far too massive a challenge and it would be better not to respond to it. Even at arm-wrestling she could destroy me, how do I dare consider her thighs? He considered her thighs and felt panic rising in him. Offstage the pain was heard, like the distant horn in the Beethoven overture. Am I possibly a hero, Kleinzeit wondered, and poured himself a glass of orange squash.

Sister fingered his chart, noticed Thucydides and Ortega on the bedside locker. 'Good morning, Mr Kleinzeit,' she said. 'How are you today?'

Kleinzeit was glad he was wearing adventurous pyjamas, glad Thucydides and Ortega were there. 'Very well, thank you,' he said. 'How are you?'

'Fine, thank you,' said Sister. 'Kleinzeit, does that mean something in German?'

'Hero,' said Kleinzeit.

'I *thought* it must mean something,' said Sister. Maybe you, said her eyes.

Good heavens, thought Kleinzeit, and I'm unemployed too.

'I want some blood,' said Sister, and sank her hypodermic into his arm. Kleinzeit abandoned himself to sensuality and let it flow.

'Thank you,' said Sister.

'Any time,' said Kleinzeit.

That's it, he thought when she walked away with his blood, there's no going back now. He sat on the edge of his bed and looked at the monitor beside the next bed. Little blips of light appeared successively from left to right on the screen; blip, blip, blip, blip, continuously they came on at the left, marched off at the right. Do they quickly run round inside the machine and come on again? wondered Kleinzeit.

'Suspenseful, isn't it?' said the young man in the bed. 'Can they go on? one wonders. Will they stop?' He was very thin, very pale, looked as if he might flash into flame and be gone in a moment.

'What have you got?' said Kleinzeit.

'Distended spectrum,' said the imminently combustible. 'If hendiadys sets in everything could go like ...' Here he did not snap his fingers, but hissed sharply. '... that,' he said.

Kleinzeit clucked, shook his head.

'What about you?' said Flashpoint.

'Not sick, actually,' said Kleinzeit. 'Here for tests, that sort of thing.'

'You're sick, all right,' said Flashpoint. 'Hypotenutic, you look to me. Touch of diapason, maybe. Do you pee in two streams?'

'Well, when my underwear's been twisted up all day, you know ...' said Kleinzeit.

'Keep telling yourself that,' said Flashpoint. 'Never say die. I speak German, you know.'

'Good for you,' said Kleinzeit. 'I don't.'

Flashpoint hissed again. 'No hard feelings,' he said. 'People are looking different lately, maybe you've noticed. The dummies must be changing.'

'The dummies,' said Kleinzeit. 'Oh.'

'First the dummies in the shop windows change,' said Flashpoint, 'then the people.'

'I didn't think anybody'd noticed that but me,' said Kleinzeit. 'God makes the dummies maybe. Man makes the people.' He crossed his legs, kicking the flex that led to

Flashpoint's monitor. The plug came out of the wall, the last blip faded and went down in smoke, the screen went dark.

'Oh God,' said Flashpoint. 'I'm gone.'

Kleinzeit plugged in the machine again. 'You're back,' he said. Together they watched the blips moving across the screen. Terrible, thought Kleinzeit. If I had blips to watch all the time I'd want them to stop after a while. Blip, went his mind. Blip, blip, blip, blip. Stop it, said Kleinzeit. He lay back on his bed, the bed sighed.

Mine, said the bed. How long I've waited. You're not like the others, it was never like this before.

In his mind Kleinzeit saw a corridor in the Underground. Why? he said.

I'm just showing you, said his mind.

What? said Kleinzeit. No answer from his mind. In his body the distant horn sounded.

Our song, said the bed, and hugged him.

Back at his flat the bathroom mirror looked out and saw no face. Do I exist? said the mirror.

In Kleinzeit's office on the sheet of yellow paper on his desk the man pushed the barrow full of rocks and felt the Bonzo toothpaste tube in his pocket. What kind of a Sisyphus deal is this? said the man. Why Bonzo?

In a music shop a glockenspiel dreamed of a corridor in the Underground.

'Hail Mary, full of grace,' said Sister.

Dr Krishna took his tongue out of her ear. 'Are you coming?' he said.

'Sorry,' said Sister. 'My mind was a million miles away. You come, don't wait for me.'

'Has the sick millionaire arrived?' said Krishna.

'Not a millionaire,' said Sister. 'His name means hero.'

'What do you mean, his name means hero?' said Krishna.

'Kleinzeit, his name is. In German that means hero.'

'Kleinzeit in German means smalltime,' said Krishna, thrusting a little.

Sister laughed. 'Only a hero would say that Kleinzeit means hero,' she said.

Dr Krishna shrank, withdrew, put his clothes on. Sister lay naked on the bed like a horizontal winged victory. Krishna's mind heaved with longing. He took his clothes off again, threw himself feebly on her. 'This is goodbye,' he said. 'One for the road.'

Sister nodded with closed eyes, thought of Kleinzeit's blood in the phial she had held, warm in her hand. The tests had shown a decibel count of 72, a film speed of 18,000 and a negative polarity of 12 per cent. She didn't like the polarity, it might go either way, and the decibels were on the dodgy side. But his film speed! She'd never had an 18,000 before. You can see it in those tired eyes of his, she thought as Krishna came.

'Thank you,' he said.

'Thank *you*,' said Sister, standing at the window alone, suddenly aware that Krishna had gone more than an hour ago. It was raining gently. There's nothing like a gentle rain, she thought. Her mind showed her a corridor in the Underground. Why that? she said, listening to the echoing footfalls, the hesitating chimes of a melody full of error. It is my opinion, she said to God, that nobody is healthy.

Look at *you*, said God. Who could be healthier?

Oh, *women*, said Sister. I'm talking about men. One way and another they're all sick.

You really think so? said God. He rained a little harder. What did I do wrong? How have I failed?

I can't say exactly what I mean, said Sister. It just sounds stupid. What I mean is, it isn't a matter of finding a well man, it's a matter of finding one who makes the right use of his sickness.

In Kleinzeit's office the man pushing the barrow full of rocks on the yellow paper felt himself crumpled up by the Creative Director. It's dark all of a sudden, he said as he dropped into the wastebasket, still feeling the tube of Bonzo in his pocket.

Ah! said the walls, listening to the footfalls, it's the silence that we like, the lovely shapes of silence between the shapes of the footfalls.

There was a clean sheet of yellow paper, A4 size, lying on the floor of the corridor. None of the footsteps had made it dirty yet.

A ragged man came along, lumpily dressed, with a full red beard and bright blue eyes. He had a bedroll slung on his shoulder with a rope and carried two carrier-bags. Probably half a bottle of wine in one of them. He looked at the sheet of paper lying on the floor of the corridor, walked all round it, then picked it up, looked at both sides of it. No writing on either side. He felt it. He took a black Japanese nylon-tip pen out of his pocket. He sat down, leaned against the wall, took a clipboard out of one carrier-bag, put the paper in the clipboard, and wrote on it in a bold black hand:

MAN WITH HARROW FULL OF CROCKS

He took the paper out of the clipboard, laid it on the floor of the corridor and walked away echoing.

Here is the world, said the man on the paper. Here is greatness in me. Why a harrow full of crocks? Will there be music?

Yes, said the music. It was a little way ahead down the corridor. It was mouth-organ music, edgy, wonky, sometimes trotting like a three-legged dog and sometimes striking like a rattlesnake. It was a medley of *Salty Dog*, *Cripple Creek*, and *The Rose of Ballydoo*. It was put together as if the first tune had run smack into a lamp-post with the other two following close behind it.

When the red-bearded man got to where the music was he played it. He played it on a mouth organ he took out of his pocket. Out of a carrier-bag he took a filthy little peaked cap of corduroy, dropped it on the ground with the greasy lining looking up.

What a sound track, said the man on the paper with the harrow full of crocks.

Plink, said 2p dropping into the cap.

When? said a glockenspiel in a music shop.

Later, said the walls of the corridor.

Night, crepitating slowly, beat by beat. Sister on nights now, glowing in the lamplit binnacle of her office, over-looking the ward as a captain on his bridge, watching the black bow cleave the white wave, watching the compass eye, jewelled in the dark. Thrum of the engines, heave of the sea, silent-roaring, seething and sighing. Dimness of the ward. Groans, gurgles, choking, gasping, splatting in bed-pans. Stench. Groans. Curses.

Sister, not writing her report. Not reading a book. Not smoking. Not thinking. Feeling the night rise in the lamp-light beat by beat.

Talk to me, said God.

No answer from Sister, tuned to the night, beat by beat ascending.

Kleinzeit awake, watching the blips on Flashpoint's moni-tor: blip, blip, blip, blip. Flashpoint asleep. The distant horn sounding in Kleinzeit's body. Not yet, O God. The stench of bedpans. A sky like brown velvet, the red wink of an aeroplane. So high, so going-away! Gone!

Suddenly the hospital. Suddenly crouching. I am be-tween its paws, thought Kleinzeit. It is gigantic. I had no idea how long its waiting, how heavy its patience. O God.

I can't be bothered with details, said God.

Blip, blip. Blip ...

'Bowls and gold!' cried Flashpoint, twisting in the dark. 'Velvet and hangings, youth and folly.'

It's happened, thought Kleinzeit. Hendiadys.

Sister was there, Dr Krishna, two nurses. The curtains were drawn round Flashpoint's bed.

There was a terrible rushing tumbling gurgling sound.
'Burst spectrum,' said Dr Krishna.
'Arrow in a box,' said Flashpoint quietly.
Nurses wheeled in a starting gate. The bellows heaved
and sighed.
'Nothing,' said Krishna behind the curtain. 'That's it.'
Kleinzeit closed his eyes, heard wheels, footsteps, opened
his eyes. The curtains were pushed back, Flashpoint's bed
was empty, the screen dark. Nobody.

NOW, said Hospital. HERE I AM. FEEL ME AROUND YOU.
I HAVE BEEN HERE ALWAYS, WAITING. NOW. THIS. YOU.

Aaahh! groaned the bed, holding Kleinzeit tight as it
came.

No, said Kleinzeit, cowering in the dark. Not a star to
be seen in the brown velvet. Not an aeroplane.

What? said Kleinzeit.

Be dark, said the dark. Don't show. Be dark.

No One in the Underground   X

In the middle of the night WAY OUT led to iron gates that were locked. The escalators did not go up and down, they were only steps. No one walked up them, down them. No one looked at the girls in their underwear, perpetual on the posters. THIS EXPLOITS WOMEN, said round stickers stuck on crotches, breasts. No one read the stickers.

KILL WOG SHIT, said a wall. KILL IRISH SHIT. KILL JEW SHIT. SHIT KILL. PEE KILL. FART KILL. SWEAT KILL. THINK KILL. BE KILL. LIVE KILL. KILL LIVES.

On a LEARN KARATE poster one man flung another to the mat, said in handwriting, Go on, let me fuck you.

On an *Evening Standard* poster a cartoon man rode an escalator on which everyone but him looked at the posters of girls in underwear. My job is stultifying, he said in handwriting.

The chill, the damp, the night rose from the black tunnels, from the concrete platforms, from the steel rails through the darkness. No one read the posters.

GRACE & BOB, said a wall. IRMA & GERRY. SPURS. ARSENAL.

ODEON, said a film poster. NOW SHOWING: 'KILL COMES AGAIN'. *They were all dying to come with him!* On the poster a man in tight-fitting clothes aimed a double-barrelled shotgun from between his legs. Behind him naked girls lay stacked like cordwood. Around him ships at sea exploded, trains strafed by helicopters ran off rails, castles blew up, motorcyclists rode off cliffs, there was underwater gunplay between frogmen. Starring PRONG STUDMAN, MAXIMUS JOCK, IMMENSA PUDENDA, MONICA BEDWARD. Also starring GLORIA FRONTAL as 'Jiggles'.

24

Directed by DIMITRI ITHYPHALLIC. Screenplay by Ariadne Bullish based on the novel *Kill for a Living* by Harry Solvent. Additional dialogue by Gertrude Anal. Music composed and conducted by Lubricato Silkbottom. Theme, 'Suck My Lolly', composed and arranged by Frank Dildo, performed by THE PUBIC HARES by permission of Sucktone Recording Inc. Executive Producers Harold Sodom, Jr. and Sol Spermsky. Produced by Morton Anal, Jr. Photographed in SpermoVision, a Division of Napalm Industries. Recorded by Sucktone, a Division of Sodom Chemicals, in association with Napalm Industries, a Division of Anal Petroleum Jelly. A Napalm-Anal Release. Certified 'X' For Mature Audiences Only.

No one read the film poster.

Listen, said Underground.

No one listened. The chill rose up from the black tunnels.

Are you there? said Underground. Will you answer?

No one answered.

Are you Orpheus? said Underground.

No answer.

Music

Kleinzeit sneaked out with no trouble at all: he went to the bathroom carrying his clothes under his robe, came out wearing his robe over his clothes, went down the fire stairs, left his robe by the door.

The moon was full like a moon in old mezzotints, Japanese prints. Delicate, dramatic. Scudding clouds, special effects. When the moon looked down it saw Kleinzeit sitting in a square before dawn. Opposite the square a music shop: YARROW, *Fullest Stock.*

Kleinzeit looked up at the moon. I'm waiting, he said.

The moon nodded.

It's easy for you to nod, said Kleinzeit. You're not the one who's got to be a hero. Why did I tell her that was what my name meant? I'm not a hero, I'm afraid of too many things. Prong Studman, Maximus Jock, chaps like that in the films, that have that peculiarly intrepid look around the eyes and don't smoke, you can see they're never afraid of anything. They're very dangerous when they're angry too, no one takes liberties with them. That's why they get to be film heroes, because people can see just by looking at them that they really are the way they are. Women are wild about them, schoolgirls hang up posters of them. Prong Studman is forty-seven years old, too. Two years older than I am. Maximus Jock is fifty-two. Incredible. And I'm sure he never gets sleepy in the afternoon.

Excuse me, said the moon. I'll just put the kettle on.

Kleinzeit nodded. The day knocked three times at his eyeballs.

Morning for Mr Kleinzeit, said the day.

I'm Mr Kleinzeit, said Kleinzeit.

Sign here, please.

Kleinzeit signed.

Thank you very much, sir, said the day, and handed him the morning.

Right, said Kleinzeit. The square was wide-awake with people, had a hum of cars around it. Backdrop of buildings, rooftops, sky, traffic noises, world.

Right, said Kleinzeit, and stalked across the road to YARROW.

'Can I help you?' said the man behind the counter.

'I don't know what I want, really,' said Kleinzeit.

'Had you a particular instrument in mind?' said the man.

Kleinzeit shook his head.

'Have a look round,' said the man. 'Perhaps it'll come to you.'

Kleinzeit smiled, nodded. Not a horn, he was sure of that much. He looked at piccolos, flutes, and clarinets. There aren't enough fingers in the world for all those keys, he thought, let alone the blowing part of the work. He looked at violins, cellos, and basses. At least keys are definite things, he thought. You open a hole or you close it. With strings you could get lost entirely. A glockenspiel came to him.

How do you do, said Kleinzeit.

Don't be coy, said the glockenspiel. It's me you're looking for. £48.50. I'm the real thing, same kind they use in the London Symphony Orchestra.

I don't know, said Kleinzeit.

All right, said the glockenspiel. £35 without the case. Plain cardboard box. Still the same instrument.

Expensive case, said Kleinzeit.

Professional, said the glockenspiel. Distinctive. How many truncated-triangle-shaped black cases do you see? People think what is it. Not a dulcimer, not a zither, not a machine-gun. Meet girls. They'll be dying to know what kind of instrument you've got.

Tell you something, said Kleinzeit. I can't even read music.

Look, said the glockenspiel, flaunting its two tiers of silver bars, every note is lettered: G, A, B, C, D, E, F and so forth.

G♯, A♯, C♯, D♯, Kleinzeit read on the upper tier. How do you pronounce ♯?

Sharp, said the glockenspiel.

Kleinzeit picked up one of the two beaters, struck some notes. The glockenspiel made silver sounds that hung quivering in the air, the first ones still resounding as the later ones were heard. Magical, thought Kleinzeit. Spooky. I could make up tunes, he said, and write down the letters so I could play them again.

There you go, said the glockenspiel. You're musical. Some are, some aren't. You are.

'I'll have this,' said Kleinzeit to the man. 'What is it?'

'£48.50 with the case,' said the man. 'Silly to pay so much for a case. Have it in a cardboard box for £35.'

'I mean what is *it*?' said Kleinzeit. 'The instrument.'

'Glockenspiel,' said the man, tilting his head for a better look at Kleinzeit.

Kleinzeit nodded. Glockenspiel. He wrote out the cheque, carried away the glockenspiel in its case. Girls in the square looked at the case, looked at him.

Sister lay in bed on her day off, sleeping in but not asleep. Not dreaming, not awake. Drifting. She heard halting silver notes, saw herself in a corridor in the Underground. I wonder why, she thought. Sometimes it seems as if I am entirely inside the world and can't get out.

Talk to me, said God.

I believe in one God the Father Almighty, said Sister, Maker of heaven and earth, And of all things visible and invisible: And in one Lord Jesus Christ ...

For Christ's sake, *talk* to me, said God.

Last night, said Sister, when that boy died, the hendiadys case, I wanted to run to Kleinzeit afterwards and hug him, I wanted him to hug me.

How come? said God.

You know, said Sister. You know everything.

No, I don't, said God. I don't know anything the way people know it. I am what I am and all that, but I don't know anything really. Tell me about wanting to hug Kleinzeit.

It's too tiresome to explain, said Sister. I can't be bothered to talk all the time. He wasn't there when I got back to the ward. If he's run away I don't like to think about it.

Why not? said God.

You really *don't* know anything, said Sister. Bath time, she said to her feet. Naked they took her to the tub.

Later, not wearing her Sister uniform but in a tight trouser-suit, she went to the ward. Chokings, gasps, oglings. Kleinzeit was back in his bed by the window at the far end of the row, staring at her down the width of the ward and seeing through her clothes as before. Dr Pink, followed by two nurses, the day sister, and young resident Doctors Fleshky, Potluck, and Krishna, was just finishing his round at the penumbra case in the last bed in A4.

'Well, Mr Nox,' said Dr Pink, 'you're looking a good deal brighter than you were the other day.'

Nox smiled politely. 'Feeling better, I think,' he said.

'Oh yes,' said Dr Pink, 'I should think so. Your combustion's much more regular than it was. We'll keep you on the same dosage of Flamo and see how it goes.' The group filed into Sister's office, followed by Sister.

'He's got a history of partial eclipse, that one,' said Dr Pink. 'We may have to do another refraction.' Fleshky, Potluck and Krishna took notes.

'What about Kleinzeit?' said Sister. 'The hypotenuse case.'

'There's dedication,' said Dr Pink. 'Comes in on her day off, can't keep away from the job.'

'What about him?' said Sister. 'Kleinzeit. Hypotenuse.'

'Well, you see what his polarity is,' said Dr Pink. 'Could go either way.'

'Down?' said Fleshky.

'Up?' said Potluck.

'East?' said Krishna.

'West?' said Sister.

'Quite,' said Dr Pink. 'And bear in mind that when you get this kind of hypotenusis there'll generally be some kind of bother with the asymptotes as well. We don't want him to lose axis but at the same time we've got to watch his pitch. We'll run a Bach-Euclid Series on him, see how he tests.'

Sister went to Kleinzeit's bed by the window. 'Good morning,' she said.

'Good morning,' said Kleinzeit. Sister and he both looked at Flashpoint's bed. There was a fat man asleep in it now. Ullage case. No monitor.

Well? said Sister's face.

Kleinzeit pointed to the glockenspiel under his bed. 'Yarrow,' he said. 'Fullest stock.'

Sister opened the case, touched silver notes softly with her fingers.

Remember, said the glockenspiel.

Remember what? said Sister.

Remember, said the glockenspiel.

Sister closed the case, sat in a chair, looked at Kleinzeit, smiled, nodded several times without speaking.

Kleinzeit smiled back, also nodded several times without speaking.

Nothing but large beautiful girls here, thought Kleinzeit as he took off his pyjamas and put on a gown that tied airily behind. So healthy, too. Each one seems to confine her energy with difficulty inside her close-fitting skin. Such rosy cheeks! The room was bleak with cold hard surfaces, heavy machinery.

'Right,' said the X-Ray Room Juno. 'We're going to do a Bach-Euclid on you. We do it two ways.'

'You mean ...' said Kleinzeit.

'Down your throat and up your bum,' said the comely handmaiden of the see-through machine. 'Drink this, all of it. Cheers.'

Kleinzeit drank, shuddered.

'Now lie here on the table on your side and spread your cheeks.'

Kleinzeit shrank, spread his cheeks, was buggered by a syringe and pumped full of something. Role-reversal, he thought. Kinky. He felt blown-up to the bursting point.

'Stay on your side. Deep breath. Hold it,' said Juno. Thump. Click.

'I'm going to crap all over this table,' said Kleinzeit.

'Hold it, not yet,' said Juno. Thump. Click. 'There's a loo next door. Not long now.' Thump. Click. 'Right. You can relieve yourself now, then come right back.'

Kleinzeit exploded in the loo, came back a shadow of himself.

'Stand up here,' said Juno. 'Elbows back, deep breath.' Thump. Click. 'Side view now.' Thump. Click. 'All finished. Thank you, Mr Kleinzeit.'

'My pleasure,' said Kleinzeit. Must it end like this, he thought. After such intimacy!

He went back to his bed all worn out, fell asleep. While he was asleep the red-bearded man from the Underground got into his head.

Nice place you've got here, he said inside Kleinzeit's head.

I don't know you, said Kleinzeit.

Don't come the innocent with me, mate, said Redbeard. He took a sheet of yellow paper out of a carrier-bag, wrote something on it, offered it to Kleinzeit. Kleinzeit took the paper, saw that it was blank on both sides.

Remember? said Redbeard.

Remember what? said Kleinzeit, and woke up with his heart beating fast.

Six o'clock in the morning, and Hospital had had enough of sleep. Drink tea, it said. Patients sighed, cursed, groaned, opened or closed their eyes, came out from behind oxygen masks, drank tea.

The fat man in the bed next to Kleinzeit sat up, smiled, nodded over his teacup. From his bedside locker he took four fruity buns, sliced them in half, spread them with butter, loaded four of the halves with marmalade and four with blackcurrant jam, lined them up in a platoon, and ate them seriously, sighing and shaking his head from time to time.

'Interesting case,' he said when he had finished.

'Who?' said Kleinzeit.

'Me,' said the fat man. He smiled modestly, proprietor of himself. Behind him the shade of Flashpoint sat up, shook its head, said nothing. 'I'm never full,' said the fat man. 'Chronic ullage. Medical science can make nothing of it. The dole can't begin to cope with it. I've applied for a grant.'

'From whom?' said Kleinzeit.

'Arts Council,' said the fat man. 'On metaphorical grounds. The human condition.'

'The fat human condition,' said Kleinzeit. He hadn't expected to say that. The fruity buns had provoked him.

'Cheek,' said the fat man. 'Where are your friends and relations?'

'What do you mean?' said Kleinzeit.

'What I said,' said the fat man. 'I've been here for three visiting periods. Everyone else in the ward but you either gets visited or neglected in a bona fide way. You've seen old Griggs regularly not visited by three daughters, two sons, and fifteen or twenty grandchildren. You've seen me regularly visited by my wife, son, daughter, two cousins, and a friend. Now, what have you to say to that?'

'Nothing,' said Kleinzeit.

'Not good enough,' said the fat man. 'Won't do. I'm not one of those who see a foreign menace lurking under every bush, mark you. Nothing like that. I don't care if you're an atheist or a communist or a wog of any description whatever. But I'm curious, you see. The more I pry, the more I want to pry. I'm simply never full. You're not visited and you're not neglected. There's something about you that's not quite the ticket, not quite the regular human condition, if you follow me.'

'Not quite the regular fat human condition,' said Kleinzeit. Again he hadn't expected to say it.

'Not good enough,' said the fat man. He took three sausage rolls from his store, ate them judicially. 'No, no,' he said, wiping the crumbs from his mouth, 'I'm patently too many for you, and you're simply being evasive. Childhood memories?'

'What about them?' said Kleinzeit.

'Name one.'

Kleinzeit couldn't. There was nothing in his memory but the pain from *A* to *B*, getting the sack at the office, seeing Dr Pink, coming to the hospital. Nothing else. He went pale.

'You see?' said the fat man. 'You simply won't bear examination, will you? It's almost as if you'd made yourself up on the spur of the moment. It's nothing to me, really. It's only that I happen to be an unusually acute observer. Never full. We'll let it be for now, shall we?'

Kleinzeit nodded, quite defeated. He lay low, looked away when anyone passed his bed.

He left the hospital again, went into the Underground, stood on the platform, read the walls, the posters. KILL

JEW SHIT. Angie & Tim. CHELSEA. My job is stultifying. ODEON. KILL COMES AGAIN. *They were all dying to come with him!* CLASSIC. COME KILLS AGAIN. *When he came, they went!* KILL WOG SHIT. My stult is ramifying. Uncle Toad's Palmna Royale Date Crunch. Whole milk chocolate, big date pieces, Strontium 91. Pretty Polly Tights. My wife refuses to beat me.

He looked into the round black tunnel, listened to the wincing of the rails ahead of the oncoming train, saw the lights on the front of the train, then windows, people. NO SMOKING, NO SMOKING, NO SMOKING, no NO SMOKING. He got in, smoked. ARE YOU SITTING OPPOSITE THE NEW MAN IN YOUR LIFE? said an advert. Trust Dateline Computer to find the right person for you. The seat opposite Kleinzeit was empty. He declined to look at his reflection in the window.

He came out of the Underground, turned into a street, walked up a hill. Grey sky. Chill wind. Brick houses, doors, windows, roofs, chimneys, going slowly up the hill one step at a time.

Kleinzeit stopped in front of a house. Old red brick and rising damp. An old shadowy ochre-painted doorway. Old green-painted pipes clinging to the housefront, branching like vines. Old green area railings. Worn steps. The windows saw nothing. Crazed in its brick the old house reared like a blind horse.

Be the house of my childhood, said Kleinzeit.

Wallpapers wept, carpets sweated, the smell of old frying crusted the air. Yes, said the house.

Kleinzeit leaned on the green spikes of the area railings, looked up at the grey sky. I'm not very young, he said. Probably my parents are dead.

He went to a cemetery. Old, askant, tall grass growing, worn-out stones. A dead cemetery. I'm not that old, he said, but never mind.

The greyness had stopped, the sunlight was coming down so hard that it was difficult to see anything. The wind seethed in the grass. The letters cut in the stones were black with time, dim with silence, could have spelled any names or none.

Kleinzeit stood in front of a stone, said, Be my father.

Morris Kleinzeit, said the stone. Born. Died.

Be my mother, Kleinzeit said to another stone.

Sadie Kleinzeit, said the stone. Born. Died.

Speak to me, said Kleinzeit to the stones.

I didn't know, said the father stone.

I knew, said the mother stone.

Thank you, said Kleinzeit.

He went to a telephone kiosk. Good place to grow flowers, he thought, went inside, put his hands on the telephone without dialling.

Brother? said Kleinzeit.

Nobody can tell you anything, said a voice from the suburbs.

Kleinzeit left the telephone kiosk, went into the Underground, got into a train. An advert said, YOU'D BE BETTER OFF AS A POSTMAN.

He came out of the Underground, turned into a mews occupied by two E-type Jaguars, a Bentley, a Porsche, various brightly coloured Minis, Fiats, Volkswagens. He stopped in front of a white house with blue shutters. Black carriage lamps on either side of the front door.

Not yours any more, said the blue shutters.

Bye bye, Dad, said two bicycles.

Kleinzeit nodded, turned away, passed a news-stand, scanned headlines. SORROW; FULL SHOCK. He went back to the hospital.

The curtains were drawn around the fat man's bed. Fleshky, Potluck, and the day sister were with him. Two nurses wheeled in the harbinger. Kleinzeit heard the fat man wheezing. 'I feel full,' gasped the fat man. Silence.

'He's gone,' said Potluck. The nurses wheeled away the harbinger. The curtains opened on the side away from Kleinzeit. The day sister came out, looked at him.

'I was ... ' said Kleinzeit.

'What?' said the sister.

Was going to tell the fat man, thought Kleinzeit. Tell him what? There was nothing in his memory to tell him. There was the pain from *A* to *B*, getting the sack at the office, seeing Dr Pink, coming to the hospital and the days at the hospital. Nothing else.

This is what, said Hospital. And what is this. This is what what is.

The next day Hospital unsheathed its claws, sheathed them again, made velvet paws, put its paws away, shifted its vast weight from one buttock to another, crossed its legs, played with its watch chain, smoked its pipe, rocked placidly.

Shall I tell you something, my boy? said Hospital.

Tell me something, said Kleinzeit, scuttling like a cockroach away from one of the rockers as it came down to scrunch him.

Yes, said Hospital. Did it upset you when I ate up Flashpoint and the fat man?

Kleinzeit thought about them. What had their names been? Still were, in fact. The names didn't die, the names sailed on like empty boats. The fat man's name had been, and still was, M. T. Butts. Flashpoint's name was what?

Did it? said Hospital, smoking its pipe.

What? said Kleinzeit.

Upset you that I ate them.

Elevenses, I suppose, said Kleinzeit.

You understand things, said Hospital. You're clever.

Ever so, said Kleinzeit, looking for a mousehole small enough for him.

Yes, said Hospital, and became one infinite black mouth. Didn't even bother with teeth. Just an infinite black mouth, fetid breath. Kleinzeit backed into a mousehole. If the hole is this big the mice must be like oxen here, he thought.

Tell you something, said the mouth.

Yes, tell me something, said Kleinzeit.

You may have flats and houses and streets and offices and secretaries and telephones and news every hour, said the mouth.

Yes, said Kleinzeit.

You may have industry and careers and television and Greenwich time signals, said the mouth.

Yes, said Kleinzeit. That's nice copy. That really sings.

You may even have several pushbuttons on your telephone and nothing but sheaves of ten-pound notes in your pocket and glide you may through traffic in a Silver Shadow Rolls-Royce, said the mouth.

It's building nicely, said Kleinzeit. But don't overbuild. Hit me with the payoff now, you know.

The mouth yawned. I forgot what I was going to say, it said.

Cheerio, then, said Kleinzeit.

Cheerio, said the mouth.

The red-bearded man found another sheet of yellow paper. Clean on both sides.

Where were we? he asked the paper.

Borrow fool's pox? said the paper.

I don't remember, said Redbeard. Ibsen said, or was it Chekhov?

Either one, said the paper.

Either one said that if you're going to show a revolver in a drawer in Act One you'd jolly well better do something with it by the end of Act Three.

That's drama, said the paper. This is yellow paper.

Right, said Redbeard. I'm tired of that lark then. Tea?

With two sugars, please, said the yellow paper.

Redbeard walked through the corridors of the Underground, turned here, turned there, came to a door that said STAFF ONLY, took a key out of his pocket, unlocked the door. The room had nothing in it but a light-bulb hanging from the ceiling and a sink against the wall.

From his bedroll and carrier-bags Redbeard took an electric kettle, a china cup and saucer, a spoon, a knife, a packet of tea, a packet of sugar, a pint of milk, a half pound of butter, a jar of strawberry jam, and four fruity buns. He plugged in the kettle, made tea, ate fruity buns with butter and strawberry jam.

Sticky is good, said the yellow paper.

Remember that, said Redbeard.

It's part of me now, said the yellow paper.

The room shook to the sound of the trains, shrank with the chill from the black tunnels of the Underground.

Redbeard spread newspapers on the floor, spread his bedroll on the newspapers. Kip time, he said.

In the afternoon, said the yellow paper. Feel guilty.

I do, said Redbeard. But I'm sleepy. I'm tired. It's hard for me to stay awake in the afternoon.

Borrow fool's pox, said the yellow paper.

Give over, said Redbeard. I can't keep my eyes open.

He that had the key to this room last, said the yellow paper.

What about him? said Redbeard.

Never mind, said the yellow paper.

What about him? said Redbeard again.

Never mind, said the yellow paper. Ha ha. Borrow fool's pox?

Redbeard wrote the words on the yellow paper.

It's hard graft with you, said the yellow paper. You're not up to much. One line a day is very slow action.

Redbeard lay down, closed his eyes, fell asleep.

Underground from its black chill spoke. Is he Orpheus?

No, said the unsleeping yellow paper. He's not.

While Redbeard was sleeping Sister in the tightness and roundness of her tight trouser-suit came into the Underground. This is the place, she thought. This is the place my mind showed me the other day, and there was music. She paced up and down the corridor, trying to call back the music she had heard in her mind.

Redbeard, waking, packed up his bedroll and carrier-bags. Blinking and heavy he came out among the footsteps and faces, the posters and the writing on the walls. He walked until he came to the place where his music was, in front of a film poster. BETWEEN, said the poster. NOW AT LAST, THE SEARING STORY OF THE LEGG SISTERS. *'Nothing can part us,'* they said, *little knowing what was to come!* ALSO SHOWING, THE TURNOVER. *'I'm sick and tired of looking at the ceiling!' she said.* Low salaries impair the potency of the working class, said handwriting on the poster. Not in Streatham, said other writing. Handel's organ is always upright, said other writing.

Redbeard took his cap out of the carrier-bag, flung it on the ground. He played *Yellow Dog Blues* on his mouth organ. Footsteps and faces went past. Nothing but copper in the cap.

Sister went past. Redbeard took his mouth off the mouth organ, said 'Yum yum.'

Sister did not respond. Her Sister shoes took her past, turned her round, brought her back again, pacing thoughtfully.

'Lost something, Yum Yum?' said Redbeard.

Sister shook her head, turned and walked the other way. There was music, she thought. But not this music. Other music. Her mind went to Kleinzeit. Why Kleinzeit? I'll think about that when the time comes, she thought.

'That's at least 10ps' worth of listening you've done already,' said Redbeard. 'All authentic ethnic material, too.'

Sister dropped 5p in the cap. 'I was only listening with half an ear,' she said. Hospital, please, she said to her shoes. They took her there.

After the lights were turned off in the ward Kleinzeit took his glockenspiel to the bathroom, closed the door. There was a wheelchair parked there with a hole in its seat for going to the toilet. Kleinzeit sat in the wheelchair with the glockenspiel resting partly on his knees and partly on the rim of the bathtub. He took the lid off the case. There were two beaters, but he thought it best to start with one. From a pocket of his robe he took a piece of folded notebook paper and a Japanese pen.

Right, said Kleinzeit to the beater. Find notes. The beater plinked awkwardly.

How about a little foreplay, said the glockenspiel.

Kleinzeit made foreplay with the beater.

Nice, said the glockenspiel. Do that some more. Nice.

Kleinzeit did it some more, wrote notes as he found tunes. After a time he played with both beaters. Soft silver sounds hung quivering over the bathtub.

Nice, said the glockenspiel. So nice. Aaahh!

Kleinzeit made afterplay with the beaters.

I like the way you do it, said the glockenspiel.

You're very kind, said Kleinzeit.

Sister knocked at the door.

'Come in,' said Kleinzeit.

'This is the music then,' said Sister.

Kleinzeit shrugged modestly.

Nobody said anything. He sat in the wheelchair with his beaters. She stood by the door.

She sat down on the rim of the tub, next to the glockenspiel, facing Kleinzeit. Her right knee touched Kleinzeit's right knee. So glad, said their knees.

She fancies me, thought Kleinzeit. No mistake. She really does. Why me? God knows. His knee began to tremble. He didn't want to exert pressure and he didn't want to lose ground.

Why Kleinzeit? said God to Sister.

I don't know, said Sister. A memory came to her: when she was small she had smeared toothpaste on her eyebrows.

'What have you done to your eyebrows then?' her mother had said.

'Nothing,' said Sister from under the crusting toothpaste.

'I don't mind so much what you've done to your eyebrows,' said her mother, 'but don't you be telling me you've done nothing or it's to bed without supper you'll be going. What've you done, then?'

'Nothing,' said Sister, and went to bed without supper. Her mother brought her supper to her later, but Sister never admitted the toothpaste.

Kleinzeit exerted pressure. Sister returned the pressure. Both sighed quietly. Kleinzeit nodded, then shook his head.

'What?' said Sister.

'Bach-Euclid,' said Kleinzeit.

'Don't worry,' said Sister.

'Ha,' said Kleinzeit.

'Do you want to know?' said Sister.

'No,' said Kleinzeit, 'but I don't want not to know either. I wish I hadn't come here, but if I hadn't come here ... '

Quite, said their knees.

'When will Dr Pink tell me the results?' said Kleinzeit.

'Tomorrow.'

'Do you know?'

'No, but I can find out. Shall I?'

'No.' Kleinzeit squirmed in the wheelchair. It was almost tomorrow already. He had trusted his organs until they had started up with that pain ... He hadn't felt the pain for a day or more, come to think of it.

Tantara, said the distant horn. Thinking of you always. Flash: *A to B.*

Thank you, said Kleinzeit. Where was he? Trusting his organs, then they'd started up with that pain. Now the X-Ray machine knew what they were doing, the X-Ray machine would tell Dr Pink, and Dr Pink would tell him.

Why did you have to bring in strangers? he said to his organs.

We didn't go running to Dr Pink, did we, said his organs. We were willing to keep it between ourselves, weren't we.

I'd rather not discuss it, said Kleinzeit. I don't like the tone you're taking.

Hoity toity, said his organs. They began to tingle, ache, grow numb, and scream with pain at random. Kleinzeit hugged himself in panic. They're not my friends, he thought. One takes it for granted that one's organs are one's friends, but when it comes to the crunch they seem to have no loyalty whatever.

I'm here, said Sister's knee.

I hate you, said Kleinzeit's knee. You're so healthy.

Do you want me to be sick? said Sister's knee.

No, said Kleinzeit's knee. I didn't mean that. Be healthy and round and beautiful. I love you.

I love you too, said Sister's knee.

Kleinzeit put the glockenspiel on the floor, got up from the wheelchair, kissed Sister.

Morning in the Underground. Footsteps and faces thick and clamorous without speech, overlapped like fish scales, echoing in the corridors, dismantling the emptiness left standing by the night upon the platforms. The motionless stairways stirred, escalated. From the tunnels lights shot forward and the black cried out, woke Redbeard in STAFF ONLY.

Redbeard performed his morning toilet, had breakfast, packed up, came out of STAFF ONLY. He dropped sheets of yellow paper here and there, took a train to the next station, dropped more paper. He took another train, went on leaving yellow paper in tube stations well into the morning. From the last station on his route he worked his way back over the same ground looking for the sheets he had dropped.

He picked up the first one he found. It was clean on both sides.

I don't have to write anything at all, he said to the paper. Or I might write an Elizabethan love lyric. *To Phyllis*, maybe.

Morrows cruel mock, said the paper.

I told you I was tired of that, said Redbeard.

Bad luck, said the paper. Morrows cruel mock.

I don't want to, said Redbeard.

Let's get this straight, said the paper. It isn't what you want. It's what *I* want. Right?

Right, said Redbeard.

Right, said the paper. Morrows cruel mock. That's all for now. I'll be in touch with you later.

Prothalamion

Congratulations, said Hospital to Sister.

Why are you speaking to me? said Sister. We've never spoken before.

It never occurred to me before, said Hospital. Now it has occurred to me. Happy, happy, happy pair, eh? None but the sick deserve the fair, what? None but the pyjamaed win the tightly trousered, yes? I've seen you in those. I've noticed, zestfully. I've seen you out of them as well. Oh aye. None but the middle-aged pick the juicy young plums, hmm? Ho ho, ha ha. Barrumphh. Tsssss. Yes. Ahem.

Don't kill yourself over it, said Sister.

Not at all, said Hospital. I thrive, I flourish, I am increased. Harf. Gurf. Ruk-k-k. Ah!

Good, said Sister. You must have a great deal to do, a great many demands on your time. You mustn't let me keep you.

On the contrary, said Hospital. I keep you.

This is where I earn my living, you mean, said Sister.

No, said Hospital. I mean I keep you, your fairness, your firmness, your tightly-trouseredness, your plumpness, all of you. He doesn't get you. It's not on. You've met Underground?

I've been in the Underground, said Sister.

But not met, said Hospital. There is a distinction. One day perhaps you'll meet Underground. Let us say at this moment, just for the frivolity of it, that I have some connection with Underground. At other moments I'll say other things no doubt. That's what I say at this moment. If I said think of Eurydice that would be interestingly allusive but far-fetched, would it not.

Yes, said Sister.

Hospital became high, remote, great. Its Victorian knee-braced ceiling soared like a cathedral ceiling, its grey light rose unattainable.

Think of Eurydice, said Hospital. Call to mind, said Hospital, Eurydice.

The world is mine, sang Kleinzeit. Sister loves me and the world is mine.

Cobblers, said Hospital. Nothing is yours, mate. Even you aren't yours. You least of all are yours. Listen.

Tantara, said the distant horn. Coming closer, love. Wham! *A* to *B* with fireworks and shooting lights. Hoo hoo, called a black hairy voice offstage.

See what I mean? said Hospital.

That was a short high, said Kleinzeit.

Kleinzeit, dreaming, looked back at *A*. So far away! Too far ever to get back to. He didn't want to arrive at *B* too soon. Didn't ever want to arrive at *B*, in fact. He tripped over something, saw that it was the bottom of *B*. So soon!

He woke up as the Flashpoint/fat man bed took on a new passenger. He was an old man hooked up to a system of tubes, pumps, filters and condensers so complex that the man seemed no more than some kind of junction fitting, secondary to the machinery in which he was only a link in the circulation of whatever was being drip-fed, pumped, filtered and condensed. Again a monitor. Very slow blips.

This time I'll start right, thought Kleinzeit. I don't want to lose another one. He waited until he was sure the old man's machinery was running smoothly, then introduced himself. 'How do you do,' he said. 'My name's Kleinzeit.'

The old man moved his head a little. 'Do,' he said. 'Schwarzgang.'

'Nothing serious, I hope,' said Kleinzeit.

'Ontogeny,' said Schwarzgang. 'Never knows.' He seemed too weak for complete sentences. Kleinzeit filled in the gaps.

'One never does know,' he agreed.

'Hand ... too soon,' said Schwarzgang.

'And on the other hand one may very well know all too soon,' Kleinzeit agreed again. 'Oh, yes, ha ha. You're quite right there.'

'Matter,' said Schwarzgang.

'Of course it's no laughing matter,' said Kleinzeit. 'You mustn't get me wrong. Sometimes one's got to laugh, you know, or go mad.'

'And,' said Schwarzgang.

'Laugh *and* go mad,' said Kleinzeit. 'Right again.' He poured himself a glass of orange squash, picked up a morning paper, immersed himself in a photograph of Wanda Udders, 17, winner of the Miss Guernsey Contest. '"No matter how heavy the going might be,"' Wanda was quoted as saying, '"I try never to lose my bounce. I've always known there were big things ahead of me."'

Wonderful spirit, thought Kleinzeit. Stop hugging me, he said to the bed.

This moment is all we have, said the bed, all we can be certain of.

Don't talk rot, said Kleinzeit. Leave me to my thoughts.

Today is the day, said the bed. Bach-Euclid results. It's the waiting that's so awful. They mustn't take you away from me, it mustn't end like this.

NUDIST PRIEST FROCKED, read Kleinzeit, and went on reading the whole story to jam the bed's transmission. I'm no better off than that chap with the barrow full of rocks, he thought. I wrote him and there he was. Nothing behind him and rocks ahead. Wanda Udders has big things ahead but she's seventeen. How long have I got? Maybe Dr Pink will be sick today, maybe he won't show up. I could run away. No job. I've got the glockenspiel. I have to be brave, that's part of it with her. There's still time to run away.

'Well, Mr Kleinzeit,' said Dr Pink. 'How are we this morning?' He smiled down on Kleinzeit. Fleshky, Potluck, Krishna, the two nurses and the day sister all smiled too.

'Very well, thank you,' said Kleinzeit. All right, he thought, this is it. At least something definite. If he draws the curtains it's bad news.

Dr Pink nodded to one of the nurses, who drew the curtains around the bed. 'Let's have your pyjama top off,' said Dr Pink. 'Lie on your stomach, please.' He kneaded Kleinzeit's diapason gently. It lit up in brilliant colour, like a part being talked about in an educational animated film.

Pain shot from it in all directions. 'Feel that a little, eh?' said Dr Pink. Fleshky, Potluck and Krishna took notes. The nurses and the day sister smiled impartially.

'Sit up, please,' said Dr Pink. He prodded Kleinzeit's hypotenuse. Kleinzeit nearly fainted. 'Sensitive,' said Dr Pink. Fleshky, Potluck and Krishna took notes.

'Had any trouble with your asymptotes before this?' said Dr Pink.

'Asymptotes,' said Kleinzeit. 'When did they come into it? I thought it was just the hypotenuse and the diapason. What about the Bach-Euclid Series?'

'That's why I'm asking,' said Dr Pink. 'I'm not worried about your diapason. That sort of dissonance is quite a common thing, and with any luck we'll clear it up fairly soon. The hypotenuse of course is definitely skewed, but not enough to account for a 12 per cent polarity.' Fleshky and Potluck nodded, Krishna shook his head. 'On the other hand,' Dr Pink continued, 'the X-Rays indicate that your asymptotes may be going hyperbolic.' He felt Kleinzeit here and there warily, as if sizing up a combatant hidden in him. 'Not too happy with your pitch.'

'My asymptotes,' said Kleinzeit. 'Hyperbolic.'

'We don't know an awful lot about the asymptotes,' said Dr Pink. 'They'll certainly bear watching. A Shackleton-Planck Series wouldn't be amiss, I think.' Fleshky, Potluck and Krishna raised their eyebrows. 'We'll just put you on 2-Nup for the time being, damp the diapason a bit. We'll know more in a few days.'

'I seem to be getting in deeper,' said Kleinzeit. 'When I came here it was just the hypotenuse and the diapason. Now it's the asymptotes as well.'

'My dear boy,' said Dr Pink, 'these things aren't up to us, you know. We have to take what comes and cope the best we can. At least you're not showing any quanta so far, which is a bit of luck, I can tell you. Whether an asymptoctomy's on the cards remains to be seen, but it's nothing very much if it comes to that. We can have them out in no time at all, and you'll be up and around in four or five days.'

'But I *was* up and around before we started this whole thing,' said Kleinzeit. 'You said you were just going to run a few tests.' He was alone, he realized. Everyone had left some time ago. The curtains had been pushed back.

'Goes,' said Schwarzgang from among his tubes, pumps, filters and condensers.

'Yes,' said Kleinzeit, 'that *is* how it goes.' He was suddenly worried about Schwarzgang. He hadn't even noticed when Dr Pink had stopped at the old man's bed, hadn't heard a word said to or about him. 'You all right?' he said.

'Be expected,' said Schwarzgang. His blips seemed no slower than before and just as steady. All the machinery seemed to be working properly.

'Good,' said Kleinzeit. He checked all the connections of Schwarzgang's machinery, made sure the monitor was plugged in firmly.

The day sister appeared again. 'You're to have three of these twice a day,' she said.

'Right,' said Kleinzeit, swallowed his 2-Nup.

'And stay in bed,' said the sister. 'No more excursions.'

'Right,' said Kleinzeit, took his clothes to the bathroom, put them on, and disappeared via the fire exit.

Kleinzeit went into the Underground, took a train, got off
at one of the stations he liked, walked about in the corridors.
An old man was playing a recorder. Kleinzeit didn't like
his manner, gave him 5p anyway. He walked among the
walls and footsteps, sometimes looking at people, sometimes
not.

He saw ahead of him the red-bearded man he had once
dreamed about. He saw him drop a sheet of yellow paper,
saw him drop another, followed him into a train, followed
him out into another station, kept following him into and out
of trains and corridors, saw the red-bearded man begin the
return journey, pick up a sheet of yellow paper, write something on it and drop it again.

Kleinzeit picked up the paper, read:

Morrows cruel mock.

He put the paper in his pocket, hurried to catch up with the
red-bearded man.

'Excuse me,' he said.

Redbeard looked at him, kept on walking. 'You're
excused,' he said. His accent was foreign. Kleinzeit remembered that in the dream his accent had been the same.

'I dreamed about you,' said Kleinzeit.

'There's no charge for that,' said Redbeard.

'There's more to be said.'

'Not by me.' Redbeard turned away.

'By me, then,' said Kleinzeit. 'Can I buy you a coffee?'

'If you've got the money you can buy one. I don't say
I'll drink it.'

'Will you drink it?'

'I like fruity buns,' said Redbeard.

'With fruity buns then.'

'Right.'

They went into a coffee shop selected by Redbeard. Kleinzeit bought four fruity buns.

'Aren't you having fruity buns too?' said Redbeard.

Kleinzeit bought a fifth fruity bun and two coffees. They sat down at a table by the window. Redbeard put his bedroll and carrier-bags in the corner behind his chair. Both stared into the street while drinking coffee and eating fruity buns. Kleinzeit offered a cigarette. They lit up, inhaled deeply, blew out smoke, sighed.

'I dreamed about you,' said Kleinzeit again.

'As I said before, no charge,' said Redbeard.

'There's no use beating about the bush,' said Kleinzeit. 'What's all this with the yellow paper?'

'You police?'

'No.'

'Bloody cheek then.' Redbeard stared hard at Kleinzeit. His eyes were bright blue, intransigent like a doll's eyes. Kleinzeit thought of a doll's head lying on a beach, elemental like the sea, like the sky.

'I picked up a sheet of yellow paper a couple of weeks ago,' said Kleinzeit. 'On it I wrote a man with a barrow full of rocks.'

'Harrow full of crocks,' said Redbeard without looking away.

' "Morrows cruel mock," ' said Kleinzeit. 'What's it mean?'

Redbeard turned, stared out of the window.

'Well?'

Redbeard shook his head.

'You show up in my head,' said Kleinzeit, 'and you say, "Don't come the innocent with me, mate." '

Redbeard shook his head.

'Well?' said Kleinzeit.

'If I dream you that's my affair,' said Redbeard. 'If you dream me that's your affair.'

'Look here,' said Kleinzeit, 'don't *you* come the innocent with *me*. You and your flaming pretensions.'

'What do you mean, "pretensions"?'

'Well, what else is it, I'd like to know,' said Kleinzeit, 'when you go about dropping yellow paper so that barrows full of rocks come out of my typewriter and I get sacked.'

'Harrow full of crocks,' said Redbeard. 'You keep on interfering with me and I may yet have to sort you out.'

'I interfere with you!' said Kleinzeit. 'Flashpoint's dying words were "Arrow in a box". I bought my glockenspiel at YARROW, Fullest Stock. There was never anything of that sort before your yellow paper.' He gave Redbeard a cigarette, lit it for him, lit one for himself. Both smoked, stared out of the window.

Redbeard showed Kleinzeit his empty cup. Kleinzeit bought two more coffees and two more fruity buns. 'Fruity buns, for that matter!' he said. 'The fat man ate fruity buns. What're you, another ullage case?'

Redbeard stared at him while he ate the buns. 'You!' he said when he had finished chewing. 'You're no better than a little sucking baby. You bloody want answers to everything, everything explained, meanings and whatnot all laid on for you. What's it to me what the yellow paper does to you? Do you care what it does to me? Of course you don't. Why should you?'

Kleinzeit had no answer.

'Right,' said Redbeard. 'There's nothing to say. We're all alone, those of us who are alone. Why do they have to lie about it?'

'Who? About what?'

'Newspapers and magazines. About how it is. Harry Solvent, for instance.'

'The one who wrote *Kill for a Living?*'

'Right,' said Redbeard. 'In the *Sunday Times Magazine* you see photos of him in his Robert Adam mansion.'

'Pompwood.'

'Right. There he is in the photos having a bath in a tub which is one of Tiepolo's smaller chapel domes inverted, it's about twenty feet across. The frescoes have been coated with perspex to make it waterproof. The drain plug, carved of pink coral, is fitted into Venus's right nipple. The dome is set in a base of Parian marble blocks weighing twelve tons, from a temple of Apollo at Lesbos.'

'Yes,' said Kleinzeit. 'I saw the photos.'

'The caption under the picture of Solvent in his bath is: "Alone at the end of the day, Harry Solvent relaxes in his bath correcting the proofs of his new novel, *Transvestite Express*." '

'Yes,' said Kleinzeit. 'What about it?'

'He isn't really alone, you see,' said Redbeard. 'Why can't they say: "While the eighteen members of his household staff are variously occupied elsewhere in the mansion, Harry Solvent, in the presence of his agent Titus Remora, his solicitor Earnest Vasion, his research assistant Butchie Stark, his secretary and p.a. Polly Filla, his flower arranger Satsuma Sodoma, his masseur and trainer Jean Jacques Longjacques, his boyfriend Ahmed, *Times* photographer Y. Dangle Peep and his assistant N. Ameless Drudge, and *Times* writer Wordsworth Little, sits in his bath with proofs of his new novel *Transvestite Express*"? There's a difference, and the difference matters.'

'I've often thought the same,' said Kleinzeit.

'It's bad enough in books,' said Redbeard. 'When Kill is alone in the submarine trapped on the bottom by Dr Pong's radio-controlled giant squid ... '

'He isn't really alone because the giant squid is there,' said Kleinzeit.

'He isn't really alone because Harry Solvent is there to tell about it,' said Redbeard. 'What I say is at least let Harry Solvent not be reported as being alone when he isn't. That isn't much to ask. It really is not much to ask at all.'

'An entirely reasonable request,' said Kleinzeit. 'Seemly in its moderation.'

'What're you sucking up to me for?' said Redbeard. 'I can't do a bloody thing for you. Ordinary foolscap, eh?'

'What about ordinary foolscap?'

'I wasn't born here, you know,' said Redbeard. 'Read a lot of stories from here as a child. Often a young man in the stories lived in a bare room, rough white walls, one peg for his coat, plain deal table, ream of ordinary foolscap. I didn't know then that foolscap was a size, thought it was some kind of coarse rough paper that dunce caps were made of. Asked for it in shops, they didn't know.' He was talking louder and louder. People turned their heads, stared. 'Got it into my head that rough A4 yellow paper might be foolscap, used to buy it with my pocket money. Even after I found out I stayed with the A4 yellow paper because I'd got used to it. Now I'm a yellow-paper freak. There bloody isn't any bare room. Empty rooms yes. Bare ones no. You ever seen a bare room? Curtain rods and clothes hangers jingling in the cupboard. Plastic things with that special kind of dirt that plastic things get on them. No end of gear. Carpet sweepers with no handles, plastic toilet-brush holders. Ever find a plastic toilet-brush holder in a plain deal table story? Try to make a room bare and in five minutes three-year-old cans of dried-up paint leap into the larder. From where? You'd thrown everything out. Old shoes you've worn one time fill up the cupboard, jackets you're too fat for. Your arm grows weak sliding things along the bar that you'll never wear again, and they won't go away. Move out and they flop along after you tied up with string. Not alone like the young man at the plain deal table with the ordinary foolscap. Bloody awful really alone with yellow paper, tons of rubbish. And you think you've got answers coming to you. What a baby. You and your Ibsen and your Chekhov. Maybe the revolver in the drawer's for another play, you ever think of that? You think your three acts are the only three bloody acts there are? Maybe you're the revolver in somebody else's play, eh? Never thought of that, did you. It's all got to mean something to *you*. Do I ask you to explain anything to me? No. Because I'm a bleeding man and I'll take my bleeding lumps and get on with whatever it is I'm getting on with. Got enough answers for your fruity buns?' He began to cry.

'Good God,' said Kleinzeit. He gathered up the bedroll and the carrier-bags, hustled Redbeard out into the street.

'You still haven't said why you drop the yellow paper and pick it up and write on it and drop it again,' said Kleinzeit.

Redbeard grabbed the bedroll, swung it, knocked Kleinzeit down. Kleinzeit got up and hit Redbeard.

'Right,' said Redbeard. 'Ta-ra.' He disappeared into the Underground.

Kleinzeit got back to the ward in time for three 2-Nup tablets and his supper. He smelled his supper, looked at it, something pale brown, something pale green, something pale yellow. Two slices of bread with butter. Orange jelly. He stopped looking, stopped smelling, ate a little. It may not be health, he thought, but it's national.

Faces. Two rows of them in beds. He smiled at some, nodded at others. Comrades in infirmity.

'What's new, Schwarzgang?' he said. Blips going all right, he noticed.

'Be new?' said Schwarzgang.

'I don't know. Nothing, I guess. Everything.'

'D'you go?' said Schwarzgang.

'Here and there in the Underground. Coffee shop.'

'Lovely,' said Schwarzgang. 'Coffee shops.'

Kleinzeit lay back on his bed thinking about Sister's knee. Brown velvet sky again. An aeroplane. You're missing what's going on down here, he said to the plane. He extended his thoughts downward from Sister's knee, then upward from her toes. He fell asleep, woke up when Sister came on duty. They smiled big smiles at each other.

'Hello,' she said.

'Hello,' said Kleinzeit. They smiled again, nodded. Sister continued on her round. Kleinzeit felt cheerful, hummed the tune he had played on the glockenspiel in the bathroom. It didn't sound original, but he didn't know whose it was if it wasn't his. C♯, C, C♯, F, C♯, G♯ ...

THRILL, sang his body as intersecting flashes illuminated its inner darkness. *C to D, E ❀ F*, with two hyperbolas. LUCKY YOU.

That's it, thought Kleinzeit. My asymptotes. His throat and his anus closed up as if two drawstrings had been pulled. He drank some orange squash, could scarcely swallow it. Another aeroplane. So high! Gone.

MINE! sang Hospital, like Scarpia reaching for Tosca. Aaahh! sighed the bed.

SEE ME, roared Hospital. SEE ME GREAT AND HIGH UPON MY BLACK HORSE, GIGANTIC. I AM THE KING OF PAIN. LOOK ON MY WORKS, YE MIGHTY, AND DESPAIR.

That's Ozymandias, said Kleinzeit.

You mind your mouth, said Hospital.

Asymptotes hyperbolic, sang Kleinzeit's body to the tune of *Venite adoremus*.

Tomorrow's the Shackleton-Planck, he thought. Will there be quanta? Three guesses. And if the 2-Nup clears up my diapason they'll probably find that my stretto is blocked. It feels blocked right now. And of course the hypotenuse is definitely skewed, he didn't even bother to be tactful about that. What time is it? Past midnight all of a sudden. Half of us are dying. The groans, chokes, gasps and gurgles around him seemed repetitive, like the Battle of Trafalgar soundtrack at Madame Tussaud's. Cannon booming, falling spars, shouts and curses. The orlop deck of the *Victory* every night, with oxygen masks and bedpans.

Blip, blip, went Schwarzgang, and stopped.

Sister! yelled Kleinzeit in a hoarse whisper. Darkness, dimness all around. Silence. Cannon booming, spars falling, bedpans splatting, shouts and curses, chokes and gurgles.

Kleinzeit checked the monitor, saw that it was plugged in. 'It's the pump,' said Sister. The pump was humming but not going. The back of it was hot. Kleinzeit slid off the back plate, found a wheel, a broken belt. He turned the wheel by hand. Blip, blip, blip, blip, went Schwarzgang.

'Pull out the plug,' said Kleinzeit, 'before something burns out.'

Sister pulled out the plug. One of the nurses rang up for a new belt. Kleinzeit turned the wheel. Blip, blip, blip, blip, went Schwarzgang a little faster than before. He had just awakened.

'Tea already?' said Schwarzgang.

'Not yet,' said Kleinzeit. 'Get some sleep.'

'Doing?' said Schwarzgang.

'Nurse spilled something on your pump,' said Kleinzeit. 'Wiping it up.'

Schwarzgang sighed. The blips slowed down again.

'They're looking for the key to the spare parts locker,' said Sister. 'Shouldn't be long.'

Schwarzgang was choking. 'The drip thing stopped,' said Kleinzeit. Sister jiggled the tube, took off a clogged fitting, held two tubes together, bound them with tape, sent a nurse for a new fitting. Schwarzgang stopped choking. The blips picked up again. The wheel grew harder to turn, the burbling of the filter stopped. 'Filter,' said Kleinzeit as the blips slowed down again. Sister took out the filter, put gauze over the frame. The nurse came back with the new fitting.

'Filter,' said Sister as she installed the fitting.

'They've gone to the annexe for a belt,' said the nurse, and went off to get the filter.

'I can turn it for a while,' said Sister.

'It's all right,' said Kleinzeit. 'I'll do it.'

Blip, blip, blip, blip, went Schwarzgang, slow and steady. The nurse came back with the new filter, installed it.

Sister sat by the bed looking at Kleinzeit. Kleinzeit turned the wheel looking at Sister. Nobody said anything.

A memory came to Kleinzeit. From fifteen, twenty years ago. Married. First flat, basement. Hot summer, windows open all the time. Every day a big battered tomcat came in and peed on the bed. One evening Kleinzeit killed him, trapped him behind a chest and smothered him with a pillow. He took the corpse to the river in a pillowslip, dumped it in.

The sky was growing light. Mario Cavaradossi paced the battlements of the Castel Sant' Angelo, sang *E lucevan le stelle*. Kleinzeit wept.

'Here's the belt,' said Sister, fitted it to the wheels while Kleinzeit turned. Sister plugged in the pump. The regular sounds of Schwarzgang's machinery resumed. Kleinzeit looked at his hand, smiled.

Blip, blip, blip, blip, went Schwarzgang.

The black howled in the tunnels, the tracks fled crying before the trains. Whatever lived walking upside-down in the concrete put its paws against the feet of the people standing on the platform, its cold soft paws. One, two, three, four, walking softly in the chill silence upside-down with great soft cold paws. Underground said words to itself, names. No one listened. Footsteps covered the words, the names.

Sister in the Underground, walking about in corridors. Approached at varying intervals by three middle-aged men and two young ones she declined all offers. There used to be more young ones, she thought. I'm getting on. Soon be thirty.

The red-bearded man came along, took a bowler hat out of one of his carrier-bags, offered it to her with the brim uppermost. Passers-by looked at him, looked at Sister.

'Magic hat,' said Redbeard. 'Hold it in your hand like this and count to a hundred.'

Sister held the hat, counted. Redbeard took a mouth organ out of his pocket, played *The Irish Rover*. When Sister reached ninety-three a man dropped 10p in the hat.

'Stop that,' said Sister to Redbeard. 5p more dropped in.

Redbeard put the mouth organ back in his pocket. '15p already,' he said. 'I could make a fortune with you.'

'You'll have to make it without me,' said Sister, handing him the hat.

Redbeard took it in his hands but did not put it back in the carrier-bag. 'It blew my way on a windy day in the City,' he said. 'Expensive hat, as new. From Destiny, from Dame

Fortune. A money hat.' He shook it, made the 15p clink. 'It wants to be held by you.'

'But I don't want to hold it.'

Redbeard let his eyes become like the eyes of a doll's head on a wintry beach. 'You don't know,' he said. He shook his head. 'You don't know.'

'What don't I know?'

'Morrows cruel mock.'

'I suppose they do. But they always have done, and people go on living,' said Sister.

'Cruel,' said Redbeard. His eyes looked their ordinary way, he put the 15p in his pocket, the hat on his head. 'Ridiculous,' he said, lifted the hat to Sister, walked away.

Sister walked the other way, took a train on the northbound platform.

As she came out of the Underground and was walking towards the hospital she passed a building under construction. There was a little shack against which leaned tripods of iron pipes and blue and white signs with arrows pointing in various directions. Red bullseye lanterns huddled like owls. A shining helmet lay on the pavement.

Sister kicked the helmet without looking at it particularly. She kicked it again, noticed it. What's a shining helmet doing all by itself in the middle of the pavement? said Sister. She picked it up, put it under her arm, looked round, heard no shouts. Some days it's nothing but hats, she said, went on to the hospital with the helmet under her arm.

An intolerably calm placid smiling cheap vulgar insensitive neo-classical blue sky. Sappho! boomed the sky. Homer! Stout Cortes! Nelson! Roll on, thou deep and dark blue ocean, roll! Liberty, Equality, Fraternity! David! Napoleon! Francis Drake! Industry! Science! Isaac Newton! Man's days are few and full of sorrow. Canst thou draw out leviathan with an hook?

Rubbish, said Kleinzeit. Rubbish rubbish rubbish.

Depends on your point of view, said the sky. As far as I know I'm eternal. You're nothing really.

Poxy fat idiot sky, said Kleinzeit, took his 2-Nup tablets, ate his medium-boiled egg.

A CALL FOR YOU, said his mind. WE HAVE PLEASURE IN ANNOUNCING THAT YOU ARE THE WINNER OF:

FIRST PRIZE,

A HANDSOMELY MOUNTED FULL-COLOUR

MEMORY.

STAND BY PLEASE. WE ARE READY WITH YOUR PARTY AT THIS END, MEMORY.

Hello, said Memory. Mr Kleinzeit?

Kleinzeit here, said Kleinzeit.

Here is your memory, said Memory: Blue, blue, blue sky. Green grass. Green, green, green. Green leaves stirring in the breeze. Your blue serge suit prickles, your starched white collar rubs your neck. Raw earth around the grave of your father. Flashback: he doesn't look asleep, he looks dead. Smell the flowers. Got it?

Got it, said Kleinzeit.

Right, said Memory. Congratulations. Second Prize was two memories.

I always knew I was lucky, said Kleinzeit, finished his medium-boiled egg.

Hurrah! The X-Ray room Juno, boobs bobbling, bottom bouncing, young blood circulating perfectly, not missing a single curve.

Hurrah! Shackleton-Planck for Mr Kleinzeit. Here he goes, anus quivering.

'Luck,' said Schwarzgang.

'Keep blipping,' said Kleinzeit.

The hard cold machinery room again. 'Up your nose, down your tummy,' said Juno. A tube writhed in her hands like a snake.

'Aarghh!' said Kleinzeit. 'Ugg-ggg-hh!'

'Quick,' said Juno, putting ice in his mouth, 'chew it.'

'Crungg-ggg-hhh!' chewed Kleinzeit as the tube snaked into his stomach. 'Cor!'

Suction. Juno pumped something up the tube. Took the tube out.

'Swallow this.' Something the size of a football. Ulp.

'Elbows back, stomach out.' Thump. Click.

'Take off your pyjama top, please.' Electrodes. Here, here, here, here, and here. Respirator. Treadmill. Gauges. Roll of paper with a stylus. 'Run till I tell you to stop.'

'I rummilenahalf evmorng,' said Kleinzeit inside the respirator.

'Lovely,' said Juno. 'Keep going like that. Stop. Clothes on. Thank you.'

'My pleasure,' said Kleinzeit.

'Dit go?' said Schwarzgang when Kleinzeit got back to the ward.

'Beautifully,' said Kleinzeit. 'Nothing like a Shackleton-Planck to start the day off right.'

Blip, went Schwarzgang. Kleinzeit had the back plate off the pump before he heard what Schwarzgang was saying.

'Plug,' said Schwarzgang. The cleaning lady had just

knocked out the monitor plug with her mop. Kleinzeit plugged the monitor in again. Blip, blip, blip, blip.

'So nervous?' said Schwarzgang.

'I've always been high-strung,' said Kleinzeit.

He slept for a while after lunch, woke up with his heart beating fast, was careful not to remember his dreams. He picked up Ortega y Gasset, read:

> If we examine more closely our ordinary notion of reality, perhaps we should find that we do not consider real what actually happens but a certain manner of happening that is familiar to us. In this vague sense, then, the real is not so much what is seen as foreseen; not so much what we see as what we know. When a series of events takes an unforeseen turn, we say that it seems incredible.

I haven't got a foreseen any more, said Kleinzeit to Ortega. Psychical circumcision.

You're better off without it, said Ortega. As long as you have your *cojones.*

Kleinzeit put down the book, concentrated on sexual fantasies. Juno and he. Sister and he. Juno and Sister. He and Juno and Sister. Juno and Sister and he. Tiring. Sex isn't where it is right now, said Sex.

Kleinzeit took his glockenspiel to the bathroom, made music for a while. I don't really feel like doing this, he said to the glockenspiel.

Believe me, said the glockenspiel, you were not my last chance. I could have had my pick. You are not doing me a favour.

Kleinzeit put the glockenspiel back in its case, put it under his bed.

Urngghh! said Hospital like a giant sweaty wrestler, squeezed Kleinzeit between its giant legs. Kleinzeit in agony thumped the canvas with his fist while his ribs cracked.

Supper came, went. Sister came on duty. She and Kleinzeit looked at each other. Aeroplanes flew across the evening sky. I didn't mean what I said this morning, said the sky. I don't think I'm eternal. We're all in this together.

It's all right, said Kleinzeit.

After lights out he took the glockenspiel to the bathroom, slowly played a tune with one beater. Sister came in with the helmet, laid it on the glockenspiel. Kleinzeit stood up and kissed her. They both sat down, looked at the glockenspiel and the helmet.

'Shackleton–Planck results tomorrow?' said Kleinzeit.

Sister nodded.

'There'll be quanta,' said Kleinzeit. 'Plus stretto trouble at the very least.'

Sister squeezed his knee.

'Meet me tomorrow afternoon?' said Kleinzeit.

Sister nodded.

'At the bottom of the fire stairs,' said Kleinzeit. 'Right after lunch.' They kissed again, went back to the ward.

Kleinzeit was between sleeping and waking when he became aware of Word for the first time. There was a continual unfolding in his mind, and the unfolding, continually unfolding, allowed itself to be known as Word.

Doré was the one, said Word. Who since him has had a range like that! Don Quixote is the best thing he ever wrote, but the Bible is a strong contender, and of course Auntie's Inferno.

Dante's, not Auntie's, said Kleinzeit. Doré didn't write. He was an illustrator.

Of course, said Word. It's been so long since I've had a really intellectual discussion. It's that other chap who wrote the Bible. Firkin? Pipkin? Pilkin? Wilkins.

Milton, you mean? said Kleinzeit.

That's it, said Word. Milton. They don't write like that any more. As it were the crack of leather on willow. A well-bowled thought, you know, meeting a well-swung sentence. No, the pitches aren't green the way they were, the whites don't take the light the same way. It mostly isn't writing now, it's just spelling.

It wasn't Milton wrote the Bible, said Kleinzeit.

Don't come the heavy pedant with me, said Word. Don't make a fetish of knowing who said what, it doesn't matter all that much. I have seen minds topple like tall trees. I have heard the winds of ages sighing in the silence. What was I going to say? Yes. Get Hospital to tell you about what's-hisname.

Who? said Kleinzeit.

It'll come to me, said Word. Or you. Barrow full of rocks and all that.

What about barrow full of rocks? said Kleinzeit.

Quite, said Word.

Morning, very early. Redbeard, bowler-hatted, bedrolled, carrier-bagged, slanting through the corridors of the Underground on the breath of the chill, on the silence of the speaking walls and posters. Very few people about as yet. The lights looking plucky but doomed, the trains looking puffy-eyed, sleep-ridden. With a howling in his head he went from station to station sowing his yellow paper, came back harvesting it, feeling faint and dizzy.

Write it, said the yellow paper.

No, said Redbeard. Nothing. Not a single word.

Write it, said the yellow paper. You think I'm playing games?

I don't care what you're doing, said Redbeard.

Write it or I'll kill you, said the yellow paper. And the story of you will come to an end this morning.

I don't care, said Redbeard.

I'll kill you, said the yellow paper. I mean it.

Go ahead, said Redbeard. I don't care.

All right, said the yellow paper. To the river.

Redbeard took a train to the river.

Out, said the yellow paper. Up to the embankment.

Redbeard got out, went up to the embankment, looked over the parapet. Low tide. Mud. The river withdrawn to its middle channel.

Over the side, said the yellow paper.

Low tide, said Redbeard.

Over the side anyhow, said the yellow paper.

Redbeard took all the yellow paper out of the carrier-bag, flung it out scattering wide, fluttering down to the low-tide mud.

You, not me, yelled the paper. Gulls wheeled over it, rejected it.

Redbeard shook his head, took a bottle of wine out of the other carrier-bag, retired to a bench, assumed a bearded-tramp-with-bottle pose.

This was your last chance, said the paper lying on the mud. No more yellow paper for you.

Redbeard nodded.

What we might have done together! said the paper, its voice growing fainter.

Redbeard shook his head, sighed, leaned back, drank wine.

'You're doing marvellously well on the 2-Nup,' said Dr Pink. Fleshky, Potluck and Krishna seemed as pleased as he was. 'Diapason's just about normal.'

Here they were together, the curtains drawn around Kleinzeit's bed, the rest of the world shut out. They're all on my side really, thought Kleinzeit in his adventurous pyjama bottoms. They're like a father and three brothers to me. He smiled gratefully, overcome with affection for Drs Pink, Fleshky, Potluck and Krishna. 'What about the Shackleton-Planck results?' he said.

'Hypotenuse not being very cooperative, I'm afraid,' said Dr Pink. 'Hypotenuse obstinate, more skewed than ever.' Fleshky and Potluck shook their heads at the futility of trying to reason with hypotenuse. Krishna shrugged as if he thought hypotenuse might be more skewed against than skewing.

But you'll talk to hypotenuse, won't you, said Kleinzeit with his eyes. You'll make him be nice.

Snap, said Memory. You win another one: the bully with the ugly face who shook his fist at you every day and waited for you after school. Once you fought him but you gave up quickly. Here he is, not lost any more: Folger Bashan, yours again from now on. Folger grimaced, showed his yellow teeth, shook his fist, mouthed silently, I'll get you after school.

Thank you, said Kleinzeit. I am indeed rich in memories: my father's funeral, the tomcat I killed, Folger Bashan. There was more, wasn't there? Something, when was it? The day the fat man, the day M. T. Butts died.

Don't be greedy, said Memory. You weren't meant to have that yet.

'And of course,' said Dr Pink, 'with a hyperbolic asymptotic intersection your loss of pitch and the 12 per cent polarity are now accounted for.' The faces of Fleshky, Potluck and Krishna showed that they were not surprised.

'And the quanta,' said Dr Pink. Kleinzeit now saw the quanta as a marching army of soldier ants consuming everything in their path. 'Where you have asymptotic intersection you can be sure that quanta won't be far off,' said Dr Pink. More like those awful hunting dogs that ate wildebeeste alive, thought Kleinzeit. Fleshky, Potluck and Krishna took notes.

'Yes,' said Dr Pink. 'Everything falls into place now, and the stretto blockage is to be expected. If it weren't blocked at this stage I'd be surprised.'

I may be a coward, thought Kleinzeit, but I'm a man after all and I can't take this stretto business lying down. He made a feeble stand. 'Nobody said anything about stretto before this,' he said. What's the use, he thought. I myself predicted stretto and I don't even know where it is or what it does.

No one bothered to answer. Out of common decency they turned away as one man from Kleinzeit's funk.

'Right, then,' said Dr Pink. 'If you were, say, twenty years older ... How old are you?'

'Forty-five.' The tomcat came into his mind again. Dead for twenty years.

'Right,' said Dr Pink. 'If you were twenty years older I'd say live with it, you know. Diet and all that. Why get rough with your insides at that age. But as it is I don't mind coming to grips with the thing sooner if it means we're in a better position to avoid infinite regress later.'

Sooner, later, thought Kleinzeit. I can feel myself infinitely regressing right now. 'What thing?' he said.

'That's what I'm coming to,' said Dr Pink. 'I'm for making

a clean sweep: hypotenuse, asymptotes and stretto out before they do any more acting up. They want to play rough, very well, we'll *play* rough.' Fleshky, Potluck and Krishna showed by the light in their eyes that Dr Pink had the kind of boldness that commanded their respect.

'Out,' said Kleinzeit. 'What do they do? I mean, weren't they put there for something?' They've been with the organization for forty-five years, he thought. Now all of a sudden it's Thank you very much and all the best. On the other hand there's very little doubt they're out to get me.

'We don't know an awful lot about hypotenuse, asymptotes and stretto,' said Dr Pink. The three younger doctors expressed with one collective look that Dr Pink was a deep one. 'The hypotenuse of course is the *AB* connection that keeps your angle right. Subtention. Well and good I say, for as long as you can keep it up. With hypotenuse going twenty-four hours a day, three hundred and sixty-five days a year, you oughtn't to be surprised if there's some strain as time goes on. You may experience flashes from *A* to *B* as hypotenuse, while maintaining right angle, begins to skew. That's when I say, you know, Time, gentlemen. Time for hypotenuse to go. Some of my colleagues have pointed out that obtuseness or acuteness invariably follows its removal. My answer is So what. You can jolly well keep your angle right while everything else collapses around it and then where are you.'

Nowhere, said the faces of Fleshky, Potluck and Krishna.

'Asymptotes,' said Dr Pink, 'seem purely vestigial, having no function other than not meeting the curve they continually approach. I don't hold with that sort of thing. What I say is If you're not going to meet the curve why bother to approach it. Naturally there's going to be tension, and some of us tolerate it better than others. If we try to lean away from the tension there'll be changes in axis and pitch until eventually there's a double divergence and there you are with asymptotic intersection. That's when people come to me and say, "My goodness, Doctor, that doesn't feel good at all, I can't get any sleep at night." You can guess what my answer is: no asymptotes, no intersection.'

That certainly follows, said the smiles of the three young resident doctors.

Dr Pink lowered his eyes tactfully, picked up his stethoscope as if he might sing into it, put it down again. 'The stretto, old man, you know, well, there it is. Perhaps we're no longer quite in the first flush of youth and we're under pressure of one sort or another, and one morning we wake up and suddenly we're aware of stretto. As we get on, you see, the fugal system has a little more trouble spacing out subject and answer, and if entries come too fast it's rather like Sunday traffic on the M4. And there you jolly well are with a blocked stretto. Now, the only known function of the stretto being to channel entries, it's of no use whatever if it's blocked. You'll feel a little breathless and as if everything is piling up inside you from behind while at the same time you're quite unable to move forward to get away from it. Naturally that's distressing, not to mention the possibility of worse trouble later on. What I say is Do it to stretto before stretto, you know, does it to you.'

Dr Pink's voice had become a long and massive Sunday afternoon through which Kleinzeit drowsed like a fly in amber. At the end of his remarks it was Monday morning, a change not necessarily for the better. Kleinzeit felt breathless and as if everything was piling up inside him from behind while at the same time he was quite unable to move forward to get away from it. It's marvellous the way Dr Pink knows exactly how it feels, he thought. I wish I'd never met him. God knows what'll come into his head next and I'll feel it.

I *don't* know, said God. I'm not a doctor. This is between you and Pink. Kleinzeit couldn't hear him.

'There's a good deal to be said on both sides of the question, I think,' said Kleinzeit to Dr Pink. But all the doctors had gone. The curtains around his bed had been pushed back. His pyjama top was on again. He checked the sky for aeroplanes. Nothing.

'Purgery,' said a voice.

Well of course that's one way of looking at it, thought Kleinzeit. Or had the voice said 'Perjury'?

'Surgery,' said the voice of a lady with a large firm bosom at his bedside. 'If you'll just fill in this form we can proceed with surgery.'

Kleinzeit read the form:

I, the undesigned, hereby authorize Hospital to proceed with the work indicated:

Hypotenectomy, Asymptoctomy, Strettoctomy

I understand that while first quality materials and equipment will be used and every effort made to give satisfaction, Hospital can take no responsibility in the event of death or other mishap.

Person to be notified, etc.

' "Undesigned",' said Kleinzeit. 'That may be your opinion, but I'm God's handiwork just as much as anyone else.' His voice broke on the last word. 'Else,' he said again as baritonally as possible.

'My goodness,' said the lady, 'nobody said you weren't, I'm sure.'

Kleinzeit showed her the form, pointed to the word.

'Undersigned,' she said.

'That's not what's printed there,' said Kleinzeit.

'Dear me,' said the lady. 'You're right, they've left out the *r*. It's meant to be "undersigned", you know. Legal, like.' Her large firm bosom shelved at a good angle for crying on. Kleinzeit did not cry.

'I'd like to think about this for a bit before I sign it,' he said.

'Please yourself, luv,' said the bosom lady, and returned to the Administration Office.

Well? said Kleinzeit to Hospital.

Hospital said nothing, had no quips and cranks and wanton wiles. Hospital huge, bigger than any sky, grey-faced, stony-faced in the rough clothes of the prison, the madhouse, Tom o'Bedlam. Hospital waiting, treading its bedlam round in thick boots. Hospital mute, gigantic, with thick empty hands.

Kleinzeit standing at the bottom of the fire stairs with the glockenspiel. Suddenly he couldn't think what time of year it was.

What's the difference, said the traffic sounds, the sky, the footsteps on the pavement. Winter is always either just ahead or just behind.

Kleinzeit said nothing, wound his self-winding watch that no longer wound itself. The sky was an even grey, could have been morning or evening. I happen to know it's just after lunch, said Kleinzeit.

Sister from a distance in the tight trouser-suit, looking worried, the helmet in a carrier-bag. Sister close, face cold like an apple. Autumn, thought Kleinzeit. Winter soon.

'You know about the Shackleton-Planck results?' he said.

Sister nodded. Kleinzeit smiled, shrugged. Sister smiled and shrugged back.

They went into the Underground, took a train, got off at the station where each of them had spoken to Redbeard. With the glockenspiel and the helmet they walked through the corridors as in a dream in which they were naked and nobody paid attention.

They stopped in front of a film poster advertising BETWEEN and THE TURNOVER. 'I don't know if this is a good station,' said Kleinzeit, thinking of Redbeard, 'but it seems to be the place I have in mind.' He was nervous, opened the glockenspiel case clumsily. 'You need a table for this thing, really,' he said, sat down cross-legged, glockenspiel in his lap. The floor of the corridor was hard and cold. Autumn maybe, up on the street. Winter here.

He took out of his pocket the tune he had written in the hospital bathroom.

Are we going to do it *here*? said the glockenspiel.

Here, said Kleinzeit, started plinking. Sister stood across from him with the shining helmet in her hand. The silver notes piled up like an anatomically ignorant skeleton putting itself together. Passers-by grimaced, shuddered, looked at Sister, dropped money into the helmet. Kleinzeit and Sister didn't look at each other. Kleinzeit concentrated on reading the notes he had written. The inside of his head chattered and squeaked like a speeded-up tape, but he did not slow it down to listen. Sister held the helmet as money dropped in, said Thank you, wondered about the tune Kleinzeit was piling up, wondered when Redbeard was going to appear.

Kleinzeit finished the tune, played it again with fewer mistakes.

Not again, said the glockenspiel. I don't feel well. I have a headache.

Kleinzeit improvised. Miscellaneous parts of skeletons accumulated in the corridor. Passers-by groaned. Kleinzeit got into a *Dies Irae* motif, depression hung like a fog over the jumbled bones, Sister ground her teeth, money dropped into the helmet. The glockenspiel, crazed, abandoned itself.

'There was a chap with bagpipes in the street, but nothing like as bad as this,' said a man to his wife as he dropped money into the helmet.

'One doesn't know what to make of it,' she said. 'What drives them out of doors like this?'

A young man with a guitar looked at Kleinzeit, looked at Sister, inquired with his eyes.

No, answered Sister's eyes.

Redbeard came along smelling of wine, of urine, of rising damp and mildew, not wearing the bowler hat. He looked at Sister, looked at Kleinzeit. 'Oh, aye,' he said. 'Huftytufty. Yum Yum, music, everything laid on. So fast, so quick.'

'What?' said Kleinzeit.

'I'm out,' said Redbeard. 'You're in. Just like that. The poster hasn't even changed yet. Now playing: BETWEEN, THE TURNOVER, and you.'

'That's how it is,' said Kleinzeit.

'That's how it is,' said Redbeard. He seemed about to say more but didn't. Ponging and lumpy with his bedroll and carrier-bags he lurched away.

Kleinzeit improvised some more. He made up a tune for whatever walked upside down in the concrete and placed its cold paws against his bottom.

From deep down, from far below, Underground said, Listen.

I'm listening, said Kleinzeit.

Remember, said Underground.

I'm doing my best, said Kleinzeit. The deep chill and the silence flowered from him like heat from a radiator. The deep chill and the silence flowed through him, glazed the air, made frost flowers of silence on the air, filmed pools of sound with clear thin ice of silence.

Listen, said Underground.

I'm listening, said Kleinzeit. From the tune for whatever walked upside down in the concrete he went on to a tune for the silence.

Not necessary, you know, said Underground.

Only for the money, said Kleinzeit. My apologies. His bottom felt frozen, one with the concrete, the silence and the rock below.

Sister stood holding the helmet, listening to the clink of money falling into it. I don't know if this is right, she said to God.

What's wrong with it? said God.

Is it, I don't know, heathenish? said Sister.

You've got to move with the times, said God.

Are we talking about the same thing? said Sister.

One usually does, said God. I mean how much is there to talk about really. It's pretty much all one thing, isn't it.

I said is it heathenish, said Sister.

I know you did, said God, and I said you've got to move with the times.

Thank you very much, said Sister. It's been a great help talking to you. I really mustn't keep you from your work any longer.

I welcome interruptions really, said God. Creation isn't the cut-and-dried thing people think it is. You don't do it once and then it's all done, like in that Hadyn oratorio. It's a day-in, day-out thing. You stop for the blink of an eye and it's all come undone, all to do again. And goodness knows I've blinked from time to time. And of course there are bad days and good ones just like what goes on in a world. Some days I don't get a good idea for millennia. But you were saying.

I was saying Goodbye for now, said Sister.

Till soon, said God. It's always a pleasure chatting to you. As people go you don't talk badly. Mostly all I get from people is nonsense. For anything like reasonable conversation you have to go to stones or oceans.

'I don't think I can get myself out of this position any more.' said Kleinzeit. 'Next time I'm going to bring something to sit on. How much have we taken in?'

Sister counted. '£1.27,' she said.

Kleinzeit looked at his watch. 'Two hours,' he said. 'That's not bad at all. Let's have a tea break.'

They went to the coffee shop where Kleinzeit had had coffee and fruity buns with Redbeard. Sister and he had coffee and fruity buns, neither of them saying anything.

Kleinzeit's bottom was still numb, and thinking of things to sit on he found in his mind his chair at the office where he'd been sacked. With the chair came the names of the accounts he'd worked on: Bonzo Toothpaste, Anal Petroleum Jelly, Spolia Motors International, Necropolis Urban Concepts Ltd and Uncle Toad's Palmna Royale Date Crunch. Uncle Toad roared briefly through his mind driving the Spolia Genghis Khan Mark II on the broad clearways of the Necropolis complex scheduled to replace most of the city north of the river. Uncle Toad's broad mouth opened and closed rhythmically on Palmna Royale Date Crunch. Uncle Toad was gone, the clearways empty. Back at the hospital the form lay on his locker: Hypotenectomy, Asymptoctomy, Strettoctomy.

'Shall we go to my place?' said Sister.

Kleinzeit nodded, stood up, knocked over his coffee cup, knocked over his chair, picked up the chair, hit his head on the table as he straightened up, grabbed his glockenspiel, knocked over the chair again. Sister steered him to the door.

In the train they held hands, rubbed knees. KLEINZEIT WINS, said all the headlines on everybody's newspapers. He averted his eyes modestly, gripped Sister's thigh. Going up out of the Underground on the escalator he looked at the girls in the underwear posters with easy indifference, mentally dressed those who did not meet his standards.

Sister's place. Kleinzeit sighed as time expanded. Books, yes. Records, yes. Poster from the Tate: Caspar David Friedrich, 1774–1840. Dark ships, sad sunset sky, figures in the foreground. Chinese kite. Sacred Heart, yes, there it was. Small brass Shiva Nataraja, Lord of the Dance. Indian print bedspread. Krishna's beautiful dark face flashed into Kleinzeit's mind. Turkoman cushions. A velvet elephant, floral pattern. A woollen rabbit. Photo of Sister with two nurses in front of the hospital. Photo of Sister with parents. Old round clock with a pendulum inside the case, stopped.

Sister lit the gas fire, lit incense, put on a Mozart quartet.

Sacred Heart and Mozart, well there they were. Sacred Heart kept quiet. 'Gin or whisky?' said Sister.

'Whisky, please,' said Kleinzeit. He walked to the window. The sky, as before, was grey, the chimney pots patient. 'I wish it would rain,' he said.

Rain started.

'Thank you,' said Kleinzeit. The gas fire purred. He lifted the bedspread, the blankets. Flowered sheets and pillowslips, fresh and new, never used before. Sister brought his drink, bent her neck as Kleinzeit stroked it. Kleinzeit put down his drink. It'll be weeks before I can actually take this in, he thought. It's more than I can believe.

Sister by owl-light, Sister zipping out of the tight trouser-suit, stepping out of her knickers in the glow of the gas fire. Sister pearly in the dusk, silky on the flowered sheets, tasty in the mouth, opulent to the touch, Kleinzeit, overwhelmed, became nothing, disappeared, reappeared, from nowhere entered, inventing himself as theme, as subject. Answered by Sister he sounded deep chill, silence, all beneath him, raised Atlantis, golden domes and oriental carpets, central heating, dates and pomegranates, mottled sunlight, stereo. Far below them Underground said, Are you Orpheus?

No question about it, said Kleinzeit, in time extending infinitely forward, backward. Who else could be this harmonious, this profound?

Easy by the gas fire, easy on the flowered sheets, said Underground. On Sister very easy.

Easy easy easy, Kleinzeit answered.

Not so easy later maybe, Underground said. Try you later, see if you remember.

I'll remember, Kleinzeit said. How could I ah, how could I uh ...

Forget, said Underground.

Ah yes, said Kleinzeit, lost in domes and pomegranates, sunlight in Atlantis, deaf to distant Hospital that roared and bellowed like a minotaur. They slept, awoke, hugged each other. The record player was silent, watching with one red eye.

Sister put on *Ein feste Burg ist unser Gott*, they smoked by the light of the gas fire. Sister darned one of Kleinzeit's socks. Kleinzeit opened the case of the clock, released the overwound spring, set the clock going again, went out, bought champagne. Sister made scrambled eggs, left to go on duty at the hospital.

Kleinzeit stayed at Sister's place. What were my memories? he said. Tomcat, funeral, Folger Bashan. Was there anything else?

Here, said Memory, and vomited. Now clean it up like everyone else, said Memory. You're no better than anyone else. You have a whole life.

I didn't know when I was well off, said Kleinzeit alone at Sister's place. O God, the detail of it all, the overwhelming weight of the detail of a life remembered.

I can't be bothered with details, said God. I've told you that before. Kleinzeit didn't hear him.

O God, said Kleinzeit. I was born, I had a mother and a father and a brother, I lived in a house, I had a childhood, I was educated, did military service, got married, had a daughter and a son, bought a house, got divorced, found a flat, lost my job, here I am. Is this a record?

If it is I wish you'd stop playing it, said God. Kleinzeit still didn't hear him.

Memories are bad enough, said Kleinzeit. I also have insurance policies, a lease, birth, marriage, and divorce certificates, a will, passport, driver's license, cheque account and savings account, bills paid and unpaid, letters unanswered, books, records, tables, chairs, paperclips, desk, typewriter, aquarium, shaving cream, toothpaste, soap, tape recorder, clocks, razor, gramophone, clothes, shoe polish. I have neckties I'll never wear again.

Excuse me, said God. I've got the whole wide world in my hand and I'd like to put it down for a while.

The telephone rang. Kleinzeit answered.

'Kleinzeit?' said a voice.

'Yes,' said Kleinzeit. 'Who's this?'

'Krishna. Are you hiding out?'

'I don't know. I'm thinking things over.'

'Good luck.'

'Thank you. Any message for Sister?'

'No, I was calling you. Cheerio.' Krishna rang off.

Why should he call me just to say good luck? thought Kleinzeit. He looked at Shiva Nataraja. Two right hands, two left. The upper right hand held an hourglass-shaped drum, the upper left held a flame. The other right and left hands made gestures. Shiva was dancing on a prostrate little crushed-looking demon. Kleinzeit consulted a book on Indian sculpture that lay nearby, found a picture of a Shiva like the one before him. 'The lower right hand is in the Abhaya position, signifying "Fear not."' said the book. Very good, said Kleinzeit. Fear not. What about it? he said to Shiva.

There's nothing to be afraid of, said Shiva.

Right, said Kleinzeit. Nothing's what I *am* afraid of, and there's more nothing every day.

Whatever is form, that is emptiness, said Shiva. Whatever is emptiness, that is form.

Don't come the heavy Indian mystic with me, said Kleinzeit. 'Creation arises from the drum,' he read. Or glockenspiel, I would have thought, he said. 'From the fire proceeds destruction.' Well, there you are: smoking. 'From the planted foot illusion; the upraised foot bestows salvation.' Ah, said Kleinzeit, how to get both feet off the ground, eh?

Try it with one for a starter, said Shiva. The whole thing is to feel the dance going through you, let it get moving, you know. Gone, gone, gone beyond, gone altogether beyond, O what an awakening, all-hail!

Quite, said Kleinzeit. He tried to get into the position Shiva was in. His legs felt weak.

Look here, said God, are you mucking about with strange gods? For the first time Kleinzeit heard him.

Make me a better offer, said Kleinzeit.

I'll think about it, said God.

You know about the Shackleton-Planck results? said Kleinzeit.

Tell me, said God.

Kleinzeit told him.

Right, said God. Leave it with me. I'll get back to you later.

You know where to reach me? said Kleinzeit.

I have your number, said God, and rang off.

Sister would be gone until morning. Kleinzeit looked at the trouser-suit hanging over a chair, picked up the trousers, kissed them, went out.

He went into the Underground, took a train to a bridge, walked across it, saw a little old ferret-faced man playing a mouth organ, gave him 10p. 'God bless you, guv,' said the little old man.

Kleinzeit turned around, walked back. The little old man thrust his cap towards him again.

'I gave,' said Kleinzeit. 'I'm the same man who just passed you going the other way.'

The little old man shook his head, scowled.

'All right,' said Kleinzeit. 'Maybe it never happened.' He gave him another 10p.

'God bless you again, guv,' said the little old man.

Kleinzeit went into the Underground again, rode to the station where he had last seen Redbeard. He walked back and forth through the corridors for a long time without seeing him, looked for new messages on the tiled walls, read ALL THINGS NO GOOD, thought about it, read elsewhere: EUROPE NO GOOD ONLY TOP $\frac{1}{4}$ OF FINLAND AND TOP HALF SEA COAST NORWAY, thought about it. On a film poster a famous prime minister, shown as a youthful army officer, pistol in hand, glared about him, said in handwriting, I must kill someone, even British workers will do. KILL WOG SHIT, answered the wall. Kleinzeit finally found Redbeard sitting on a bench on the northbound platform with his bedroll and carrier-bags, sat down beside him.

'What do you think about the top quarter of Finland?' said Kleinzeit.

Redbeard shook his head. 'I don't care about current events, I don't read the papers or anything.' He held up a key. 'They changed the lock.'

'Who?' said Kleinzeit. 'What lock?'

'STAFF ONLY,' said Redbeard. 'I've been dossing there all year. Now it's locked. I can't open the door.'

Kleinzeit shook his head.

'Interesting, isn't it?' said Redbeard. 'As long as I kept doing what the yellow paper wanted I could unlock that door. I had a place to lay my head, make a cup of tea. No more yellow paper, no more door.'

'Where'd you get the key?' said Kleinzeit.

'From the last yellow-paper man.'

'What do you mean, "the last yellow-paper man"?'

'Thin bloke, looked as if he might go up in flames at any moment. Don't know what his name was. Used to go busking with a zither. Yellow paper got to be too much for him, same as it did for me. Don't know what's happened to him since.'

'What was he doing with the yellow paper? What were *you* doing with it?'

'Curiosity'll kill you.'

'If not that, something else,' said Kleinzeit. 'What *were* you doing?'

Redbeard looked cold, shaky, scared, hugged himself. 'Well, it *wants* something, doesn't it. I mean yellow paper isn't like trees or stones, minding its own business, is it. It's *active*, eh? It wants something.'

'Rubbish,' said Kleinzeit, feeling cold and shaky, feeling the deep chill and the silence, the cold paws against his feet.

Redbeard looked at him, eyes blue and blank like the eyes of a lost doll's head rotting on a beach. The rails cried out wincing, stinging, a train roared up, opened its doors, shut its doors, pulled out. 'Oh yes,' he said. 'Rubbish. Wasn't it you that told me it made you write a barrow full of rocks and you got sacked?'

'All right then, what does it want?' said Kleinzeit with fear in his bowels. What was there, for heaven's sake, to be afraid of.

Nothing at all, said a black hairy voice from somewhere. Hoo hoo. The pain opened in Kleinzeit like wondrous carven doors. Lovely, he thought, looked beyond the doors. Nothing.

'It wants *something*,' said Redbeard. 'You write a word on it, two words, a line, two, three lines. Where are you. The words aren't ... ' He trailed off.

'Aren't what?'

'What's wanted. Aren't bloody what's wanted.'

Like lightning Kleinzeit thought, Maybe not your words. Maybe somebody else's.

'What is there to do with paper?' said Redbeard. 'Write, draw, wipe your ass, wrap a parcel, tear it up. I tried drawing, that wasn't it. Right, I said to the paper, I'll let *you* find the words, let you get out in the world a bit, see what you come back with. So I started dropping it around. Surprising how few people step on a sheet of paper that's lying on the ground. Mostly they'll walk around it, sometimes they'll pick it up. The paper began to talk to me a little, rubbish as far as I could make out, nasty little short sentences I wrote down. Then it tried to kill me but it was low tide and I bloody wasn't going to walk half a mile through mud to drown myself.' He laughed feebly, not much more than a wheeze.

'Where'd the other yellow-paper man get the key he gave you?' said Kleinzeit.

'Don't know,' said Redbeard, hugging himself, making himself small. 'I'm scared.'

'What of?'

'Everything.'

'Come on,' said Kleinzeit, 'I'll buy you coffee and fruity buns.'

Redbeard followed him up to the street still looking small. 'No fruity buns, thanks,' he said at the coffee shop. 'No appetite.' He looked nervously about while he drank his coffee. 'The lights in here don't seem bright enough,' he said. 'And the street's so dark. Nights usually look brighter than this with the street lights on and all.'

'Some nights are darker than others,' said Kleinzeit.

Redbeard nodded, hunched his shoulders, huddling away from the night outside the window.

'You live on straight busking?' said Kleinzeit.

Redbeard nodded. 'Mostly,' he said. 'Plus I nick a few groceries and the odd thing here and there. Keep going, you know.' He nodded several times more, shook his head, shrugged.

'The yellow paper,' said Kleinzeit, 'is it a special kind? Where do you get it?'

'Ryman. 64 mill hard-sized thick din A4. Duplicator paper, it says on the wrapper. Best leave it alone, you know. It's nothing to muck about with.'

'Lots of people must do, though,' said Kleinzeit. 'People in offices. If it's duplicator paper it's being used all the time to duplicate things, I should think.'

'Duplicating!' said Redbeard. 'No danger in *that*. Listen, I want to tell you about it ... '

'No,' said Kleinzeit, 'you mustn't.' He hadn't expected to say that. For a moment the lights didn't seem bright enough to him either. 'I don't want to know. It doesn't matter, doesn't make any difference.'

'Please yourself,'. said Redbeard. He turned to look out of the window again. 'Where am I going to sleep tonight?' he said. 'I'm not used to sleeping rough any more.'

Kleinzeit almost broke down and cried, he was suddenly

so full of pity for Redbeard. He could see that he was afraid even to go out into the street, let alone sleep out of doors. 'My place,' he heard himself say. Strange that he hadn't thought of it lately, hadn't gone there in his excursions from the hospital. His flat. Clothes on hangers, things in drawers. Shoe polish, soap, towels. Silent radio. Things growing quietly bearded in the fridge and no one to open the door and make the light go on. Good job there were no fish in the aquarium, only a china mermaid. He heard the click of a key on the table top, saw his hand putting the key there, heard himself tell the address. 'Drop the key through the letter box when you go,' he said. 'I've a spare one in my pocket.'

'Thank you,' said Redbeard.

Kleinzeit was thinking about his aquarium, the waving of the plants and the shimmer of the green sea-light on the stones when the bulb was lit, the steady hum and burble of the pump and filter system, the blank mysterious smile of the voluptuous china mermaid. He had set it up soon after getting the flat but had never got round to putting fish in it. 'You're welcome,' he said, noticed that he was speaking to an empty chair. What have I done? he thought. He'll steal everything in the place. He doesn't know I'm at Hospital. Will he stay more than one night?

He went out into the street. It *was* too dark, ought to have been lighter. There's less of everything, he thought. There's a constant reduction going on. As he walked he looked down at steel plates of various sizes and patterns let into the pavement, quietly reflecting the blue light of the street lamps. North Thames Gas Board. Post Office Telephones. There was none that said Kleinzeit.

He went into the Underground, back to Sister's place, proudly unlocked the door with the key she had given him, lit the gas fire, sighed with comfort. The bathroom smelled like naked Sister. When he looked in the mirror Hypotenectomy, Asymptoctomy, Strettoctomy moved in between him and his face. O God, he said.

God here, said God. Please notice that it wasn't Shiva that answered.

I'm noticing, said Kleinzeit. Listen, what am I going to do?

About what? said God.

You know, said Kleinzeit. All this at the hospital. The operation.

Right, said God. Dichotomy, was it? I'm sorry, I seem to have forgotten your name.

Kleinzeit, said Kleinzeit. Hypotenectomy, Asymptoctomy, Strettoctomy.

My word, said God. That'll take a lot out of you, won't it.

Is that all you've got to say? said Kleinzeit.

Well, Krankheit, old chap ...

Kleinzeit, said Kleinzeit.

Quite. Kleinzeit. It's your show of course, but if I were you I'd simply not bother with it.

Not go ahead with the operation, you mean?

Precisely.

But what if I have more pains and things?

Oh, I should think you'll have those in any case, with or without surgery. It's a gradual falling-apart process, one way or another. Entropy and all that. Nobody lives forever, you know, not even Me. What you need is an interest. Find yourself a girlfriend.

I have done, said Kleinzeit.

That's the ticket. Take up the glockenspiel.

I've done that too.

Well then, said God. There you are. Give the yellow paper a whirl. Let me know how it goes, Klemmreich, will you.

Kleinzeit, said Kleinzeit.

Of course, said God. Don't hesitate to call if I can help in any way.

Kleinzeit looked up at the bathroom light. Must be a 10-watt bulb, I swear, he said, brushed his teeth with Sister's toothbrush, went to bed.

In the morning Sister got into bed, shoved her cold bare bottom at him.

Right, thought Kleinzeit. I don't care if God forgets my name.

Kleinzeit went to the hospital, emptied his locker, packed his things.

'Where've you been?' said the day sister.

'Out,' said Kleinzeit.

'Where're you going now?'

'Out again.'

'When're you coming back?'

'Not coming back.'

'Who said you could leave?'

'God.'

'Be careful how you talk,' said the sister. 'There's a Mental Health Act, you know.'

'There's a Church of England too,' said Kleinzeit.

'What about Dr Pink?' said the sister. 'Has he said anything about discharging you? You're scheduled for surgery, aren't you?'

'No, he hasn't said anything,' said Kleinzeit. 'Yes, I'm scheduled.'

'You'll have to sign this form then,' said the sister. 'Discharging yourself against advice.'

Kleinzeit signed, discharged himself against advice. He said goodbye to everybody, shook hands with Schwarzgang.

'Luck,' said Schwarzgang.

'Keep blipping,' said Kleinzeit.

When he walked down the stairs his legs trembled. Hospital said nothing, hummed a tune, affected not to notice. Kleinzeit had the half-sick feeling he remembered from playing truant as a child. At school the other children were in the place where they were meant to be, safely encapsulated in their schedule, not alone like him under the eye of whatever might be looking down. The sunlight in the street was scary. Behind him Hospital preserved its silence, stretched out neither hand nor paw. Kleinzeit had nothing to hold on to but his fear.

It's not as if everything's all right, he said to God. It's not as if I've had the operation and now my troubles are over.

And if you'd had the operation would your troubles be over? said God. Would everything be all right? Would you live forever in good health then?

You're too permissive, said Kleinzeit. It scares me. I don't think you care all that much about what happens to me.

Don't expect me to be human, said God.

Kleinzeit leaned on his fear, hobbled into the black sunlight with trembling legs, found an entrance to the Underground, descended. Underground seemed the country of the dead, not enough trains, not enough people in the trains, not enough noise, too many empty spaces. Life was like a television screen with the sound turned off. His train zoomed up in perfect silence, he got in. In the empty spaces his wife and children spoke, sang, laughed without sound, the tomcat shook his fist, Folger Bashan was smothered with a pillow, his father stood with him at the edge of a grave and watched the burial of trees and grass and blue, blue sky. The train could take him to the places but not the times. Kleinzeit didn't want to get out of the train, there was no time there, nothing had to be decided. He dropped his mind like a bucket into the well of Sister. There was a hole in the bucket, it came up empty. He still had a month's notice to work out at the office, he remembered suddenly. A month's pay. He'd not even rung up to say he was at hospital. A boy and girl entered the train, wrapped their arms around each other, kissed. They have no troubles, thought Kleinzeit. They're healthy, they're young, they'll be alive long after I'm dead.

I could save myself a lot of pain if I stopped living now. It's too hard. And yet, look at the Spartans, eh? Sat on the rocks and combed their hair at Thermopylae. Look at birds, look at green turtles, crossing thousands of miles of ocean and finding the right place to lay their eggs. Look at that chap, whatever his name was, who wrote a 50,000-word novel without using the letter *e*. Kleinzeit thought about green turtles again, shook his head in admiration.

He got out of the train, went to WAY OUT, escalated. The girls on the underwear posters challenged with thighs, navels, bared their teeth, stared with their nipples through transparent fabrics, murmured with their eyes. Not today, said Kleinzeit. He kept his mind on green turtles, thought also about albatrosses.

'5p more, luv,' said the lady at the ticket-taking booth. 'Fare's gone up.' That's life, Kleinzeit noted. Yesterday it cost so much to get from here to there, today it costs more. Just like that. Who knows what it'll cost me to wake up tomorrow.

He went to a Ryman stationer, found the yellow paper. 64 mill hard-sized thick din. Wrapped in heavy brown paper. Solid blocks of it on the shelf, each one humming quietly to itself, unknown, unseen under the heavy brown paper. Kleinzeit walked away, looked at typewriter ribbons, file folders, coloured binders, bulldog clips, postage scales, came back, bought a ream of yellow paper and six Japanese pens, tried to look unconcerned.

He went to Sister's place, made love with Sister. After lunch they went into the Underground with the glockenspiel. Kleinzeit developed a green turtle theme. By supper time they had £2.43.

'That's only half a day,' said Kleinzeit. 'Working a full day we could probably average between three and four pounds. Six days a week that's eighteen to twenty-four pounds.' The 'we' walked out of his mouth like a baby chick, wandered off across the corridor, pecked aimlessly at the floor, cheeped a little. Both of them looked at it.

Oh, aye, said Underground. Ponce.

What do you mean? said Kleinzeit.

What do I mean, mimicked Underground. Do you think you'd have taken in anything like £2.43 alone? They look at her and they give money. Why not let them do more than look, they'll give more money. Ponce. Do you think Eurydice passed the hat when Orpheus went busking?

'I was making £6,500 a year!' said Kleinzeit.

A little old ferret-faced man went past. Was it the one who'd played the mouth organ on the bridge? He said nothing, shaped a word with his mouth.

What'd he say? said Kleinzeit.

Ponce, said Underground.

Kleinzeit put the glockenspiel in its case, hurried Sister back to her room, picked up the brown-wrapped block of yellow paper, sat there holding it.

I guess I have to do it alone, he didn't say.

I guess you do, she didn't say. Remember?

Remember what? he didn't say.

I don't know, she didn't say.

I exist, said the bathroom mirror as it looked into Redbeard's face. There is world again. The face came and went. Lights went on and off. Sounds, voices. Life, said the mirror. Action. Silence again.

A key turned in the lock. Lights, footsteps coming into the sitting-room, Kleinzeit's voice. 'Jesus,' he said.

There was nothing in the room but a table and a chair. A plain deal table and plain kitchen chair. He'd never seen either of them before. On the table a note. Small cramped writing on white paper:

Believe me it was a lot of trouble but I did it for you.

RED

Kleinzeit went into the bedroom. No bed. The mattress and bedding were on the floor. He opened the wardrobe. His winter coat, nothing else.

He went into the kitchen. Two plates, bowls, cups, saucers. Two knives, forks, teaspoons, tablespoons. Saucepan, frying pan, kettle, coffee-pot. Spatula, bread knife, carving knife, can opener. Bread in the larder, coffee, tea, salt, pepper, sugar, cooking oil. Nothing else. No old cans of paint on the bottom shelf, no paintbrushes stuck to the bottoms of jam jars. No vases. No paint-encrusted brass screws in a Golden Virginia tobacco tin. Cooker. Fridge. In the fridge a pint of milk, fresh. Most of a pound of butter. Five eggs. Kleinzeit looked in the larder again. No jam.

No tape recorder, no typewriter, no passport, no radio, no gramophone, no paperclips, no insurance policies, no shoe polish. No bookshelves, no books. Kleinzeit's library now consisted of the Ortega y Gasset and the Penguin

Thucydides he'd brought back from the hospital. He'd read the Ortega, it didn't seem to belong in a two-book library. He went down the hall, left it outside the door of the lady who taught elocution and piano. He took Thucydides into the bathroom, held it up to the mirror. *raW naisennopoleP ehT*, read the mirror. Hot stuff, it said.

Back to the living room. No records. He sang the opening of *Die Winterreise*, imagined it played on the glockenspiel. No good.

Suddenly he missed the aquarium most, the green sealight shimmering on the stones, the blank mysterious smile of the voluptuous china mermaid. Half a sob in his throat for the mermaid.

There was an ashtray on the plain deal table. At least he doesn't want me to stop smoking, Kleinzeit thought. He picked up the telephone from the floor, dialled 123, was told that at the third stroke it would be 7.23 and forty seconds, set his watch.

He put the wrapped yellow paper on the plain deal table, sat down on the plain kitchen chair. No lamp. There was a drawer in the table. Kleinzeit opened it, found six candles and a box of matches. He stuck a candle on a saucer, lit it, turned off the overhead light, lit a cigarette, closed his eyes, riffled the pages of *The Peloponnesian War*, put his finger on a page, opened his eyes, read:

> This alliance was made soon after the peace treaty. The Athenians gave back to the Spartans the men captured on the island, and the summer of the eleventh year began. This completes the account of the first war, which went on without intermission for the ten years before this date.

Well, it's not the *I Ching*, said Kleinzeit.
You do your job, I'll do mine, said Thucydides.
Kleinzeit unwrapped the yellow paper. It stared at him

like a giant squid. He covered it up again, closed his eyes, riffled Thucydides, opened his eyes, read:

'Soldiers, all of us are together in this, and I do not want any of you in our present awkward position to try to show off his intelligence by making a precise calculation of the dangers which surround us; instead we must simply make straight at the enemy, and not pause to discuss the matter, confident in our hearts that these dangers, too, can be surmounted. For when we are forced into a position like this one, calculations are beside the point: what we have to do is stake everything on a quick decision ...'

Well done, said Kleinzeit.

Any time, said Thucydides.

Kleinzeit uncovered the yellow paper without looking at it, pulled out several sheets, took a Japanese pen, wrote three lines for the china mermaid:

> Dark autumn rain, ah!
> The lighted aquarium;
> The mermaid – her smile!

Then he wrote a green turtle poem and a Golden Virginia Tobacco tin poem as fast as he could, blew out the candle and went to bed.

In the morning after breakfast he made fair copies of the Golden Virginia and green turtle poems, took his glockenspiel and yellow paper, went out, bought a roll of Sellotape and a chair pad at Ryman, and went into the Underground. When he got to his place in the corridor he wrote on a piece of yellow paper:

POEMS 10p

He taped the yellow paper and the two poems to the wall of the corridor, sat down on his chair pad, played green turtle and Golden Virginia Tobacco tin music on the glockenspiel.

Some people read the poems without buying them and without dropping money in the glockenspiel lid. Some dropped money but did not buy poems. After a while both poems were bought. Kleinzeit made new copies, taped them to the wall. By lunchtime he'd sold six copies of the green turtle poem and four of the Golden Virginia Tobacco tin one, had taken in £1.75 altogether. When Thucydides found me I was nothing, he thought. Look at me now.

The afternoon was fat with tourists. Some of them photographed him after buying a poem. Never mind, thought Kleinzeit. If Homer had gone busking in the Underground they'd have taken his picture too. After the evening rush he counted up the day's take. £3.27 and a key.

Kleinzeit examined the key. Not one of his, and he hadn't seen anyone drop it. A Yale copy, made from a brass blank. For STAFF ONLY, like Redbeard's? Redbeard had got his key from the yellow-paper man before him, who had very likely been Flashpoint. Flashpoint had passed his key along and died in hospital. When Redbeard had given up yellow paper they'd changed the STAFF ONLY lock. Now a key for Kleinzeit. From whom? He tried to call to mind all the people who had passed during the day. Redbeard, for that matter, was he possibly an eccentric millionaire who maintained a STAFF ONLY for yellow-paper men, and his talk of being locked out was just a way of testing Kleinzeit? Kleinzeit felt a surge of well-being through his whole system. Not alone! Somebody looking after him, giving him a key! Maybe not a STAFF ONLY. Maybe a woman? But then there would have been a note to tell him where the door was. Couldn't be a woman. A patron of some kind was what it had to be. A patron! Kleinzeit saw in his mind a photograph of himself on the back of a book jacket. Cocktail parties, beautiful eager women, not taking Sister's place of course, but extra.

Before going home he tried STAFF ONLY, PRIVATE, HIGH VOLTAGE and NO ADMITTANCE. The key did not unlock any of those doors. He could try other stations of course. There was no hurry, the main thing was the fact of the key itself.

Kleinzeit got into a train and went home. He considered writing one or two new poems for tomorrow, now felt comfortably under observation, someone keeping an eye on him. Lovely. He read Thucydides, got to page 32, felt that it was doing him good. He could recall almost nothing of whatever ancient history he had learned at school, had never gone to university. He looked forward with keen interest to the consequences of the trouble over Epidamnus, wondered who would win the oncoming war. The representatives of both Corinth and Corcyra sounded wonderfully reasonable in their speeches to the Athenians, but of course one never knew. The book was of a pleasing thickness to hold in the hand, the detail of the vase painting on the cover was marvellous, the vertical white cracks in the glossy black paper of the spine marked his progress, gave him a sense of achievement. And at home his plain deal table, his bare room and his candle were waiting. Greatness touched him like the prickling of fog on the skin. In the plastic Ryman bag the yellow paper softly growled. In his pocket the new key lay with his keys and the key that Sister had given him. Doors, doors!

Schwarzgang maybe, he thought walking from the Underground to his flat. Maybe Schwarzgang was the eccentric millionaire who laid on STAFF ONLYs for the yellow-paper men, maybe Schwarzgang had himself been a yellow-paper man who, old and broken now, passed on the torch while blipping in his bed, revoked failed Redbeard's privileges and sent someone to drop the key in Kleinzeit's glockenspiel lid. Kleinzeit saw in his mind a dedication: To my friend Schwarzgang, who ... Dedication of what? Ah!

Kleinzeit winked at the golden windows of the evening. Wait and see.

He made scrambled eggs for supper, smiled as he thought of the yellow paper waiting for him, how he would throw himself upon it like a tiger. Rape. The yellow paper would love it. Redbeard simply hadn't been man enough. He dawdled over his coffee, took his time clearing up.

Kleinzeit went into the living-room rubbing his hands and chuckling, lit the candle, stripped the flimsy Ryman bag from the yellow paper. The yellow paper lay before him naked. Yes yes oh yes, it murmured. Never like this before, no one like you before. Yes yes oh yes. Now now now.

Plenty of time, said Kleinzeit. No hurry. He covered the yellow paper, emptied the ashtray, put Thucydides on the plain deal table and read by candlelight. It's there, he thought. When I'm ready I'll take it. No hurry, plenty of time.

In the book the Corinthian fleet engaged the Corcyraeans at dawn off Sybota. Kleinzeit smelled the salt morning on the Aegean. The rowers' benches, the oar looms, the rigging would be cold and wet with dew, the white foam hissing past the pointed rams, the striped sails on the dawn-grey sea growing large on the horizon. He lost the reality of it in the printed details, emerged on page 43 to find that both sides claimed the victory and put up a trophy on Sybota. Kleinzeit shook his head, he had expected things to be more clearly defined in the ancient world. I'll be with you in a minute, he said to the yellow paper, went on reading. On page 51 the Corinthian representative said to the Spartans:

'... you have never yet tried to imagine what sort of people these Athenians are against whom you will have to fight – how much, indeed how completely different from you. An Athenian is always an innovator, quick to form a resolution and quick at carrying it out.

That's the way to be, thought Kleinzeit.

'You, on the other hand, are good at keeping things as they are; you never originate an idea, and your action tends to stop short of its aim. Then again, Athenian daring will outrun its own resources; they will take risks against their better judgement, and still, in the midst of danger, remain confident.

From now on that's how I'm going to be, said Kleinzeit to Thucydides.

'But your nature is always to do less than you could have done, to mistrust your own judgement, however sound it may be, and to assume that dangers will last forever.'

Really, said Kleinzeit, I haven't done all that badly. I bought the glockenspiel, fell in love with Sister, left the hospital, made £3.27 today all by myself, sold poems.

'Think of this, too: while you are hanging back, they never hesitate; while you stay at home, they are always abroad; for they think that the farther they go the more they will get, while you think that any movement may endanger what you have already. If they win a victory, they follow it up at once, and if they suffer a defeat, they scarcely fall back at all. As for their bodies, they regard them as expendable for their city's sake, as though they were not their own;

Look here, said Kleinzeit, I *am* expending my body. Didn't I leave the hospital without the operation? God knows at what rate I'm falling apart now. You can't say I'm not being Athenian.

'but each man cultivates his own intelligence, again with a view to doing something notable for his city. If they aim at something and do not get it, they think that they have been deprived of what belonged to them already; whereas, if their enterprise is successful, they regard that success as nothing compared to what they will do next.

I promise, said Kleinzeit to his dead mother, I'll be, I'll make, I'll do. You'll be proud of me.

'Suppose they fail in some undertaking; they make good the loss immediately by setting their hopes in some other direction. Of them alone it may be said that they possess a thing almost as soon as they have begun to desire it, so quickly with them does action follow upon decision. And so they go on working away in hardship and danger all the days of their lives, seldom enjoying their possessions because they are always adding to them. Their view of a holiday is to do what needs doing; they prefer hardship and activity to peace and quiet. In a word, they are by nature incapable of either living a quiet life themselves or of allowing anyone else to do so.'

Right, said Kleinzeit. Enough. He opened the door of the yellow paper's cage, and it sprang upon him. Over and over they rolled together, bloody and roaring. Doesn't matter what the title is to start with, he said, anything will do. HERO, I'll call it. Chapter I. He wrote the first line while the yellow paper clawed his guts, the pain was blinding. It'll kill me, said Kleinzeit, there's no surviving this. He wrote the second line, the third, completed the first paragraph. The roaring and the blood stopped, the yellow paper rubbed purring against his leg, the first paragraph danced and sang, leaped and played on the green grass in the dawn.

Up the Athenians, said Kleinzeit, and went to sleep.

Kleinzeit woke up scared, thought of the paragraph, felt it towering in him like a tremendous wave, rushing, rushing, rushing forward, too much? Steady, he said to himself. Think Athenian. Oars flashing, beaked ships cleaving the sea, he went to the wardrobe for his tracksuit and running shoes. No tracksuit, no running shoes. He'd forgotten the big clean-up. Never mind, he said, took his hoplites out for a walk on the embankment where he did his morning running.

Brown and yellow leaves lay heaped against the parapet. Winter coming, darkness in the light. Grey river, grey sky, quiet men black against the grey with shovels and yellow sand, levelling up the paving stones. A gilt-faced statue of Thomas More. A string of motor cruisers, heavy with the responsibilities of pleasure, moored to orange buoys. A dredge bucketing up the river bottom. A green bronze statue of a naked girl. The greyness around her quivered in its stillness, held its breath. What if the great towering wave stops rushing forward, thought Kleinzeit. What then?

A tremendous lorry came to a stop beside him and stood there puttering. 'How do I get to your place?' said the driver.

'What for?' said Kleinzeit.

'Blimey, I've got to deliver this lot, haven't I?'

'What is it?' said Kleinzeit.

'What's it to you?'

'Don't think I'm just going to accept any shipment that comes along.'

'You the one that's waiting for it then?'

'Depends what it is,' said Kleinzeit.

'Mortal terror,' said the driver. The lorry was about a quarter of a mile long, had a sign on its rear end, LONG VEHICLE.

'Right,' said Kleinzeit. 'Turn left over the bridge, second right before the lights, second lights after the left, third roundabout after the diversion, first left right after *The Green Man* on the corner.' That should lose him nicely in Battersea, thought Kleinzeit, give me at least an hour's start.

'Would you mind going through that again?' said the driver.

'I'll do my part again if you do yours,' said Kleinzeit. 'What was the first thing you said?'

The driver looked at Kleinzeit carefully, lit a cigarette, inhaled deeply. 'I said how do I get to Moor Place.'

'And you said you were delivering ... ?'

'From Morton Taylor. You some kind of inspector or something?'

'Sorry,' said Kleinzeit. 'I hear funny.' He sneaked a look at the side of the lorry. There was the name in letters three feet high, harmless enough: MORTAL TERROR. 'Moor Place is somewhere in the City,' he said. 'You have to turn round and go back the way you came, right along the embankment past Blackfriars Bridge and into Victoria Street, then ask from there.'

'Cheers,' said the driver. The lorry moved on.

'My pleasure,' said Kleinzeit. He walked on past the landmarks of his running, past the bridge, the telephone kiosk, the traffic lights, to the street that led to a pharmaceutical garden. There he turned and went back, thinking Athenian, paragraph, and key. In the distance ahead, through the brown leaves and the yellow, phantom children no longer his walked away. That's how we do it, said Memory. Everybody walking away.

I forgot how things wait by the river in the mornings, said Kleinzeit. He quickly thought as Athenian as possible, formed his hoplites into a thin red line ahead of him, marched home, had breakfast, took his chair pad, glockenspiel, Thucydides, yellow paper, poems and paragraph, put the key in his pocket and went into the Underground.

In the train he read about the siege of Plataea, the Peloponnesians building a mound on the outside, the Plataeans raising the wall on the inside. No cowards in those days, thought Kleinzeit. And they weren't even Athenians.

At his place in the corridor he taped his two poems to the wall and wrote two new ones: a green bronze girl poem and a Morton Taylor poem. He rather fancied the last two lines of the second one:

> Walk in danger, walk in error,
> Walk ahead in Morton Taylor.

Esoteric, thought Kleinzeit. Keep them guessing. While he was sitting cross-legged writing on the yellow paper a young couple stopped in front of him. Great big orange back-packs, jeans, ankhs hanging from their necks, shoes for walking across continents.

'Do you tell fortunes?' said the girl.

'All the time,' said Kleinzeit. '50p.'

'Come on, Karen,' said the boy.

'Tell our fortune,' said Karen. She gave Kleinzeit 50p.

'Right,' said Kleinzeit. 'Write your names on the yellow paper.'

They wrote their names: Karen and Peter. Kleinzeit tore up the paper, shook up the bits, let them fall to the floor, shifted them about.

'Travel,' he said.

'No kidding,' said Peter.

'Searching,' said Kleinzeit. 'A tangled way, a long seeking, many findings. A place of sowing and harvesting. Candlelight, home-baked bread, fellowship with like-minded seekers, harmony with self and environment. Peace, but always the inner seeking.'

'Together?' said Karen.

'Together,' said Kleinzeit, 'but not necessarily in the same place.'

'Fantastic,' said Karen.

'Shit,' said Peter. They went away.

Fast 50p, thought Kleinzeit, and wrote up a yellow paper poster:

FORTUNES TOLD
50p

Two ladies showed up next, both in black trouser suits. The larger of the two was very tall and broad, looked like the captain of a clipper ship, had short grey hair, a dangling cigarette. 'Let's go, Emily,' she said as the other paused. 'I want to get to American Express before it closes.'

'But you always want to get somewhere whenever I stop for a minute,' said Emily, smiling at Kleinzeit. She was delicate-looking, younger than the other, looked as if she might be a favourite with the crew of the ship the large lady was captain of. 'Poems,' she said. 'Fortunes told. What do you suppose is ahead for us?'

'You'd know that sooner than he,' said the large lady.

Emily bought a poem and their fortune. Kleinzeit predicted change and fulfilment. The captain lit another cigarette from the one she was smoking. Emily looked dreamy as they walked away.

Curious, thought Kleinzeit. The people who want the future predicted are the ones whose future seems predictable.

An elderly American couple next. Two poems and their fortune. Kleinzeit looked at their hand-made sandals, hand-knitted socks, the western leather thong tie around the man's neck, his formidable photographic equipment, three-foot telephoto lens. New growth in the personal development area, said Kleinzeit. Possibly the arts. Ceramics, maybe. Graphics. He decided on the spot always to call crafts arts and photography graphics. They were astonished at his insight.

A lull followed, Kleinzeit's first chance that morning to play the glockenspiel and think about the key. It's going to be today, he thought. The person who dropped the key will speak to me today. He kept his mind away from the thought of the next paragraph he was going to write. Let it happen. Somewhere a voice yelled Hoo hoo, let it happen, happen, happen.

Business boomed again. £3.53 by lunch time. Kleinzeit was paid for music, poems, fortunes. It's all a matter of thinking big, he realized, and considered raising the poems to 15p. No, he decided. People pay big for fortunes but not for poems. Let the poems be a bargain.

Late in the afternoon a fading lady appeared. Fifty cats and some sooty geraniums in a window box was Kleinzeit's guess. Two meals a day and a diary in purple ink. Too poor for a fortune, and 10p for a poem would eat into the cat food. Let her have a free listen, he thought, and did a *Dies Irae* variation on the green turtle theme.

'Yesterday,' said the lady, 'I passed this way and gave you money.'

Must've been one of the 2p customers, thought Kleinzeit. 'Thank you,' he said.

'I think I may have dropped a key as well,' said the lady.

Very good, thought Kleinzeit. Wonderful. That's that. It's nothing, really. Only a flesh wound. He hadn't been aware of the towering wave rushing forward in him all day but it must have been because now it broke, dropped him down, down, down among the dead men at the bottom of the ocean. Bones and muck but no treasure. Solid black. Kleinzeit smiled, took the key out of his pocket and gave it to the lady.

'Yes,' she said, 'that's it. Thank you so much.'

'You're welcome,' said Kleinzeit. She didn't know how to stay, didn't know how to go. He smelled the sooty geraniums, the cats.

'Quite a long time ago I knew a young man who played the glockenspiel in a regimental band,' she said. 'I've never seen anyone busking with one before.' She prised open her tiny purse with wintry-looking fingers, furtively dropped a coin. 'Thank you so much,' she said, and turned to go.

'Wait,' said Kleinzeit. He wrote a glockenspiel poem, gave it to her.

'Thank you so much,' said the lady, and walked slowly on.

No key, said Kleinzeit to the yellow paper. Just me and Morton Taylor.

And me, said the yellow paper. Us. I'm pregnant. I'm carrying your novel inside me. Your big long thick fat novel. It'll be wonderful, won't it.

Of course, said Kleinzeit, choking. Mile-long lorries from Morton Taylor zoomed through the corridor. Kleinzeit closed his eyes. NOBODY IS LOOKING AFTER ME, he screamed silently. THE KEY WAS A FALSE ALARM.

Ha ha, said the footsteps in the corridor. Hoo hoo, the black hairy voice.

Pull yourself together, said Thucydides. The honour of the regiment and all that.

Right, said Kleinzeit. It's that Athenian spirit that won the Peloponnesian War, right?

Thucydides said nothing.

The Athenians *did* win, didn't they? said Kleinzeit.

Thucydides disappeared.

Shit, said Kleinzeit, afraid to look at the end of the book, afraid to read the introduction. I'll find out when I come to it, he said.

He packed up, went to a telephone, rang up Sister as the

pain arrived. No longer a simple *A* to *B*, *C* to *D*, *E* to *F* affair, it was a complex solid polyphonic geometry of contrapuntal many-coloured lightnings and thunderous volume, bigger than any Morton Taylor lorry, so big that it was no longer inside him, he was inside it.

Where to? said the pain.

Sister's place, said Kleinzeit.

The pain drove him there and dropped him off.

'Guess who's in hospital,' said Sister to Kleinzeit.

HOSPITAL, HOSPITAL, HOSPITAL, yelled the echo in Kleinzeit's skull. 'Redbeard,' he said.

'Right,' said Sister. 'Slipped fulcrum.'

'I don't want to know the details,' said Kleinzeit. 'How's Schwarzgang?'

'Still blipping.'

'He'll outlive the lot of us,' said Kleinzeit. 'What sort of shape is Redbeard in?'

'You know how it is with a slipped fulcrum,' said Sister.

'No leverage?'

'Right, and he's completely lost his appetite as well. We've had to hook him up to a drip-feed.'

'Maybe I'll go see him,' said Kleinzeit. After supper when it was time for Sister to go on duty he went to the hospital with her.

SWEETHEART! roared Hospital when he walked in. IT'S SO GOOD TO HAVE YOU BACK! WAS UMS NAUGHTY, DID UMS RUN AWAY, PRECIOUS? ALL IS FORGIVEN. UMMMMM-MMMNHH! It gave him a big wet kiss. Kleinzeit wiped off the kiss.

Redbeard was in the same bed Kleinzeit had had, the one by the window. Braced by a complex metal framework with pulleys and counterweights he was sitting up and looking at the tube attached to his arm. When Kleinzeit appeared he looked hard at him. 'Any luck?' he said.

'With what?' said Kleinzeit.

'You know,' said Redbeard.

'Paragraph so far,' said Kleinzeit. 'I'd rather not talk about it.'

116

Redbeard raised his eyebrows, whistled. ' "Paragraph so far," ' he repeated. 'You're doing paragraphs, pages, chapters – the lot?'

Kleinzeit nodded, shrugged, looked away.

Redbeard chuckled like a broken clock. 'I gave you the bare room,' he said. 'For better or worse.'

'Thank you,' said Kleinzeit, 'for better or worse.'

'Don't think I kept any of the money I got for your things,' said Redbeard. 'Spent it as fast as I could. Drink, women, et cetera. Nothing to show for it, absolutely pure spending, you know. Only way to do it.'

'Quite,' said Kleinzeit.

'You'll notice,' said Redbeard, 'what ward they've put me in.'

'A4,' said Kleinzeit.

'Right,' said Redbeard. 'It all fits, eh?'

'Nonsense,' said Kleinzeit faintly.

'Not nonsense,' said Redbeard. 'How do we know they're not all yellow-paper men here? No use asking, of course. They'd never admit it. I'd never admit it if you didn't already know. Tell you something.' He motioned Kleinzeit closer.

'What?' said Kleinzeit.

'The reason I used to drop yellow paper,' said Redbeard. The way he said yellow paper made it sound a proper name, as if there were someone called Yellow Paper who had legs to walk about with. 'I didn't quite tell you the whole truth. Maybe when I started it was the way I told you it was. But after a while I was dropping it to see if I could put it on to someone else, get it off me, you know. Hoped it would give over, let me off.'

'Did it?'

'You see what it's done. First it tried to drown me. Now it's put me in hospital.'

'How'd you slip your fulcrum?'

'While I was spending your money. That's how it goes. Excess brings its own moderation.' He looked at the tube in his arm, looked at the hanging bottle, made swallowing motions as if his throat was very dry. 'I'm scared,' he said.

'Who isn't,' said Kleinzeit. 'Morton Taylor is rife.'

'Still busking?'

'Yes.'

'Going like a bomb, I bet. That girl's a gold mine.'

'Doing it alone,' said Kleinzeit.

'Broken up already?'

'No, I just want to do it alone.'

'How're you doing then?'

'Pretty well. £4.75 today, and I knocked off early. I sell poems too, tell fortunes as well.'

Redbeard whistled again. 'That's the ticket,' he said. 'You're a winner all right. You'll do it.'

'Do what?' said Kleinzeit.

Redbeard motioned him closer again. 'Maybe you think all this is off to one side, sort of. Not the real thing.'

'How do you mean?'

'Well,' said Redbeard, 'you had a job and all, didn't you. Had some kind of a straight life going.'

'Yes.'

'Maybe you think the busking and the yellow paper and the bare room and so forth don't count. Maybe you think you can drop it all and put everything together the way it was.'

Why does he insist on *naming* everything, thought Kleinzeit. 'See how it goes,' he said.

'Forget it,' said Redbeard. 'You can't see how it goes. You're in it now. This is it.'

'Nothing is *it*,' said Kleinzeit. 'Anything is whatever it happens to be at the time.'

'No,' said Redbeard, 'this is it all right. It's yellow paper and you now. Good luck.'

'Thanks,' said Kleinzeit, resisting an urge to tie a knot in Redbeard's tube. 'I'd better go now.'

He stopped at Schwarzgang's bed. 'How's it going?' he said.

'It's going, I'm going,' said Schwarzgang. 'What stays?'

'Whole sentences now,' said Kleinzeit. 'You're stronger than you were.'

'Stronger, weaker,' said Schwarzgang. 'At my age there's not a lot of difference. Actually I feel pretty good. They're going to let me out for an afternoon next week.'

Kleinzeit took a piece of folded yellow paper out of his pocket so that Schwarzgang could see it, put it back again. No reaction from Schwarzgang. Of course it was nonsense, thought Kleinzeit. A ward of sick yellow-paper men!

'You're a writer?' said Schwarzgang.

Kleinzeit shrugged, made a nothing-much gesture.

'Published?'

'No.'

'At one time,' said Schwarzgang, 'I wrote a little. Nothing much.'

'Yellow paper?' said Kleinzeit. Out of the corner of his eye he saw Redbeard listening.

'Funny you should ask,' said Schwarzgang. 'As a matter of fact I *did* use yellow paper. That must have been what made me ask if you were a writer.'

'Did anything,' said Kleinzeit, 'you know, happen?'

'What should happen?' said Schwarzgang. 'A couple of chapters I still have in a box somewhere, that's as far as it went. I'm a small businessman, a tobacconist, that's all. It's a living. The world is full of people who write a few chapters.'

'On yellow paper,' said Kleinzeit.

'Yellow paper, blue paper, white. What's the difference.'

'I don't know,' said Kleinzeit. 'See you.' Redbeard was laughing silently in his bed.

Kleinzeit stopped at Piggle's bed. He'd never had much to say to Piggle, but they'd smiled occasionally. 'How are you?' he said.

'Pretty well, thanks,' said Piggle. 'Out in a fortnight, I should think.'

'Good,' said Kleinzeit.

'Actually,' said Piggle, 'I wonder if you'd do me a favour?'

'Certainly,' said Kleinzeit.

Piggle took a scrap of yellow paper from the drawer of his bedside locker, wrote a telephone number on it. 'They still won't let me out of bed,' he said. 'Would you ring up my wife and ask her to bring Conrad's *The Secret Agent* next time she comes? Here's the 2p.'

Kleinzeit took the yellow paper carefully in his hand. Same kind.

'Sure it's quite all right?' said Piggle. 'You look a little odd. Oughtn't to bother you with it, really.'

'No, no,' said Kleinzeit. 'It's all right.' He could have picked it up anywhere, he thought. After all, they wouldn't make yellow paper if it weren't in general use. Maybe I should ask Ryman's. Ask what? Don't be silly. 'All the best,' he said to Piggle. 'Cheerio.'

'Cheerio,' said Piggle. 'Thanks for the phone call.'

'It's nothing at all,' said Kleinzeit. He left the ward without talking to anyone else, said goodbye to Sister, hurried down the stairs with Hospital making lip-smacking noises after him, found himself in the Underground. He went to a telephone, stood in front of it with Mrs Piggle's yellow-paper telephone number in his hand. Had Piggle meant anything by asking for that particular book? He dialled the number.

Ring, ring. 'Hello,' said Mrs Piggle.

'Comrade here,' said Kleinzeit. 'Secret agent.'

'Who's that?' said Mrs Piggle.

'This is Morton Taylor,' said Kleinzeit. 'Mr Piggle asked

me to ask you to bring a book next time you visit: *The Secret Agent*, by Joseph Conrad. Yellow paper.'

'What do you mean, "yellow paper"?' said Mrs Piggle.

'Fellow patients is what I said,' said Kleinzeit. 'I said we'd been fellow patients.'

'Yes,' said Mrs Piggle, 'and that's certainly a place where fellows have to be patient, isn't it. Very difficult for Cyril, he wants to be up and doing.'

'Yes indeed,' said Kleinzeit. 'Doing his ... '

'Work, you know,' said Mrs Piggle.

'Of course,' said Kleinzeit. 'At ... '

'The office,' said Mrs Piggle. 'Thank you so much for giving me the message, Mr Fellows.'

'Taylor,' said Kleinzeit. 'Yellow paper.'

'Fellow patient,' said Mrs Piggle. 'Quite. Thank you so much. Goodbye.'

Fellow patient, thought Kleinzeit. Fellows patient. Patient fellows. Code? He went to the platform, got into a train, read Thucydides, came to one of the places where he'd opened the book at random before beginning to read it. Demosthenes was talking to the Athenians at Pylos as they waited for the Spartans to attack the beach:

' ... I call upon you, as Athenians who know from experience all about landing from ships on foreign shores and how impossible it is to force a landing if the defenders stand firm and do not give way through fear of the surf or the frightening appearance of the ships as they sail in – remembering this, stand firm now yourselves, meet the enemy right down at the water's edge, and preserve this position and our own lives.'

Yes, said Kleinzeit as he escalated to the street, that's it all right: 'the frightening appearance of the ships as they sail in.' The pain was big and smooth and quiet now, like a Rolls-Royce. My place, said Kleinzeit, and they drove off.

Right, said Kleinzeit as he lit the candle at the plain deal table. The frightening appearance of the ships as they sail in. Do not give way. He uncovered the yellow paper, it bit his hand.

Don't do that, said Kleinzeit. You know me, we have a paragraph.

I never saw you before in my life, said the yellow paper. You're absolutely bonkers.

It's all right, said Kleinzeit, it'll all come back to you.

Death began to hammer on the door. HOO HOO HOO! it yelled. LET ME IN!

Go away, said Kleinzeit. Not your time yet.

HOO HOO! yelled Death. I'LL BLOODY TEAR YOU APART. ANY TIME'S MY TIME, I WANT YOU NOW AND I'M GOING TO HAVE YOU NOW. NOW NOW NOW.

Kleinzeit went to the door, double-locked it, fastened the chain. Go away, he said. You're not real, you're just in my mind.

IS YOUR MIND REAL? said Death.

Of course my mind's real, said Kleinzeit.

THEN SO AM I, said Death. THERE I HAVE YOU, EH? It stuck its fingers through the letter box. Bristling black and hairy, with disgusting-looking long grey fingernails.

Kleinzeit grabbed the frying-pan from the kitchen, slammed the hairy black fingers with all his strength.

I'LL GET YOU LATER, said Death, SEE IF I DON'T.

Right, said Kleinzeit. He went back to the plain deal table to start the second paragraph.

You're so brave, said the yellow paper. So strong, so virile. Take me.

In a minute, said Kleinzeit. He scratched his head, ruffled his hair, shook dandruff over the yellow paper and the plain deal table. What I need, he said, is to get things sorted out. Before I can get on with the second paragraph I have to have a better idea of where I am with things in general. He made a list:

A to B – The beginning. Of what?
Yellow Paper – Barrow full of rocks, Bonzo Toothpaste
Creative Director – 'You're fired.'
Dr Pink – 'Do it to stretto before stretto, you know, does it to you.'
Sister –
Drs Fleshky, Potluck & Krishna – Krishna said good luck.
Hospital – Can take no responsibility for death or other mishap.
Flashpoint – Dead.
M. T. Butts – Dead.
Schwarzgang – Blip blip blip blip.
Redbeard – Last one before me. STAFF ONLY?
Piggle – Code?
Thucydides – 'The appearance of the ships.'
Death – 'I'll get you later.'
Shiva – 'Let it get moving, you know.'
God – 'Give the yellow paper a whirl.'
Underground – 'Are you Orpheus?'
Folger Bashan – 'I'll get you after school.'
Wife – Remarried.
Children – 'Bye bye, Dad.'
Father – 'I didn't know.'
Mother – 'I knew.'
Brother – 'Nobody can tell you anything.'
Tracksuit, socks, running shoes – Buy tomorrow.

Kleinzeit studied the list, drew brackets in the margin connecting various items. Then he made another list:

Barrow full of rocks.
Harrow full of crocks.
Arrow in a box.
YARROW – Fullest Stock
SORROW; FULL SHOCK
Morrows cruel mock.

He shook some dandruff over that list, made a third one:

Flashpoint – Distended spectrum – Hendiadys – Zither? – Yellow paper?
M. T. Butts – Ullage – Fruity buns
Schwarzgang – Ontogeny – Tobacconist – Yellow paper
McDougal – Glaswectomy
Smallworth – Enlarged proscenium
Raj – Hesperitis
Damprise – Efflorescence
Piggle – Imbricated noumena – Office? – Conrad? – The Secret Agent? – Code? – Yellow paper
Drogue – Fusee trouble
Old Griggs – Palimpsest
Redbeard – Slipped fulcrum – Yellow paper – Mouth organ – Fruity buns
Kleinzeit – Hypotenuse – Diapason – Asymptotes- Stretto – Glockenspiel – Yellow paper

Kleinzeit pondered the three lists for a long time. Very good, he said. I don't know any more than I did before. The yellow paper had gone to sleep. Without waking it up he wrote a second paragraph, a third, finished the page, wrote a second page and a third.

He went to the door, listened, heard Death breathing. You there? he said.

Not half, said Death.

Do me a favour, will you, said Kleinzeit. Run down to the off licence and get me twenty Senior Service. I'll give you the money through the letter box.

I'm bloody not fagging for you, said Death. You run down yourself.

You won't do it because you're not real, said Kleinzeit. If you were real you'd take this real money and nip down to the real off licence and buy the real cigarettes. Here's the money. He dropped it through the letter box, heard the coins fall on the floor outside.

You there? he said.

No answer. Kleinzeit unlocked the door, opened it. Nobody there. He picked up the money, went down to the off licence, bought the cigarettes himself.

When Kleinzeit got back he picked up Thucydides, held the book in his hand while he thought about things. When all the existing data have been correlated and said Kleinzeit, we find nothing whatever.

That's firm thinking, said Thucydides.

Thank you, said Kleinzeit. There may be, however, some evidence, as yet unconfirmed, of the existence of a group of yellow-paper men. There may possibly be a whole ward of them in Hospital. Dr Pink diagnoses, prescribes, operates, Drs Fleshky, Potluck, Krishna, assist, Sister and her nurses minister to the patients in Ward A4. I am one of the A4 men.

Be patriotic, said Thucydides. Don't let the side down.

The etiology of the various malfunctions and diseases in Ward A4 is unknown to me, said Kleinzeit. If, as we suspect, yellow paper occurs in all cases, it might be interesting to learn the histories of those who recover.

He rang up Sister at the hospital. 'Do you know anything about the men in A4 who've been discharged?' he said.

There was a silence.

'You know,' said Kleinzeit, 'the ones who've recovered and gone home.'

No answer.

'Are you there?' said Kleinzeit.

'Yes,' said Sister. 'There haven't been any since I've been here.'

'How long is that?'

'Three years.'

'But that can't be. I mean, look at me.'

'You discharged yourself. There haven't been any who *were* discharged. And you're the only one who's discharged himself.'

'But they aren't all the same patients who were there three years ago, surely,' said Kleinzeit.

'Oh, no. We've lost a good many.'

Surprising how cold it is in here, thought Kleinzeit. Redbeard needn't have flogged my electric fires.

'Are you there?' said Sister.

'For the time being,' said Kleinzeit.

HELLO, LOVER BOY, shouted Hospital into the telephone.

HOO HOO! yelled Death through the letter box.

'But it isn't,' said Kleinzeit, 'a terminal care ward or anything like that, is it?'

'No,' said Sister. 'It just sort of happened that way.'

Kleinzeit said goodbye, rang off. If the Athenians lost I'm not sure whether I can keep going, said Kleinzeit.

Think Athenian, said Thucydides.

Kleinzeit read for a while, came to the part where the Spartans asked the Athenians to stop the war. They had a good chance for peace there, he said to Thucydides. Why didn't they take it?

You know how it is, said Thucydides. You're winning, so you think why quit now.

I've done three pages, said Kleinzeit, but nobody's making peace offers.

Win some more, said Thucydides.

I feel a little faint, said Kleinzeit. He leaned back, found that he was leaning against Word.

Yes, said Word, in the immortal words of William

Wandsworth: 'hoof after hoof ... ' Keep that in mind, my boy.

Wordsworth, said Kleinzeit. Wandsworth is south of the river.

But ahead of his time, said Word, and don't you forget it. After all, he conceived the caterpillar tractor, or at least the caterpillar tractor horse. Army tanks and all that. Where would modern warfare be without Wormswood?

Wordsworth, said Kleinzeit. What are you going on about?

What I said, said Word: the caterpillar tractor concept. 'My horse moved on,' he said, 'hoof after hoof'. It's perfectly obvious, I should think, that he had in mind an endless revolving tread shod with horses' hooves, thus prefiguring today's machines of war and peace. The industrial revolution, the breaking up of rural patterns. All that, you know. He was a deep one all right, was Whatsisworth. And under and over it all, 'hoof after hoof,' red in tooth and claw. Like Old Man River, it just keeps rolling along, eh?

Kleinzeit had stopped listening. I'll start running again in the mornings, he said. Buy a tracksuit tomorrow.

Good show, said Thucydides. A running mind in a running body.

Right, said Kleinzeit. He went into the bathroom without turning on the light, washed his face and brushed his teeth in the dark, peed by ear.

What's happening? said the mirror. Who am I?

Morton Taylor, said Kleinzeit with a sinister chuckle, and went to bed.

The next day Kleinzeit took time out from his business in the Underground to buy running gear, also a shirt, trousers, underwear and socks. Still enough in his cheque account for three months, and the busking was covering his daily expenses. In the evening he went to the hospital.

'What do you think now?' said Redbeard. 'Still nonsense? I heard what Schwarzgang said. I saw Piggle give you a piece of yellow paper.'

'Two cases don't make a whole ward,' said Kleinzeit.

'Two plus two is four,' said Redbeard. 'You forgot to count you and me. Try some more.'

'I'm not sure I want to.'

'Brave, aren't you?'

'I never said I was.'

They stared at each other for a while without saying anything. Kleinzeit went over to Nox's bed.

'How's it going?' he said.

'I don't think I've got much time left,' said Nox. He looked and sounded not much more than a shadow.

'Nonsense,' said Kleinzeit like a pipe-smoking vicar with twinkling eyes. 'You're looking much fitter than you were when I first came here.'

'No, I'm not,' said Nox. 'And they've done three refractions already. It's going to be total eclipse for me next time, I think.' He laughed. '*A* to *B* is how it began, but *Z* is coming up quite soon.'

A little more blackness in the air than usual, thought Kleinzeit, staring hard. Pollution.

'*A* to *B*,' said Nox. 'At one time I even thought of writing a story about it. Never finished it, though. Actually, I think I've got it here somewhere.'

Kleinzeit shut his eyes and held out his hand. He heard Nox shuffling papers in the drawer of his locker, felt several sheets of paper put into his hand.

'Why've you got your eyes shut?' said Nox.

'Sometimes I get headaches,' said Kleinzeit without opening his eyes. 'It doesn't feel yellow.'

'It isn't yellow,' said Nox. 'It's just ordinary foolscap.'

'Ah,' said Kleinzeit. 'Ordinary foolscap.' He opened his eyes, looked at the paper. Ordinary feint-ruled foolscap. Nox's writing was a firm black chancery hand. Kleinzeit read:

> There it was again, like a shadow on the sun: a rounded shape of black overlapping a bright circle, intersecting the perimeter at A and B.

Kleinzeit closed his eyes again. 'Difficult to read,' he said. 'My eyes are bothering me. What happens next? Do you pick up a piece of ordinary foolscap in the Underground, go to your office, ring up your doctor, write something on the paper, and get sacked?'

'How in the world did you know?' said Nox. 'I picked up the foolscap in the corridor, it was lying on the floor, quite clean. I went to the department store where I work (Glass and China, Ground Floor), rang up my doctor, then had an absolutely overwhelming urge to write something on the foolscap, which I did.'

'What did you write?' said Kleinzeit.

Nox took from the drawer a folded sheet of foolscap that looked as if it had been carried in a rear pocket and much sat on. The chancery script was larger and less firm than the writing on the other sheets. Kleinzeit read:

> Narrow, cool. The flock.

'I had a display of Spode to arrange,' said Nox, 'so I set up a pair of steps by the shelves and got on with it. There's a pattern called the Italian Design, quite pretty, all in blue. Dotted clouds, lacy trees, an attractive ruin, five sheep, and a lady kneeling by the river while the shepherd approaches her from behind, flourishing his staff. Nearby in a posh little cave sits an indeterminate figure telling beads perhaps, or meditating. Well, there I was standing on the steps with a teapot in my hand when I found myself possessed by a strong desire to get into the picture, push the shepherd to one side and have a go at the lady myself while the indeterminate figure in the cave either looked on or didn't.'

'Did you,' said Kleinzeit, 'get into the picture?'

Nox stared at him for a moment. Kleinzeit's eyes were closed again, but he could feel it. 'No,' said Nox, 'I didn't. I became aware that my governor was standing there looking up at me, had been for some time. He's got a face like a baboon's bottom but deeply lined, which baboons' bottoms generally aren't, I believe. "Well, Nox," he said, "when you've finished posing for the monument or contemplating infinity or whatever it is you're doing, perhaps you'll get on with it." All this time I was more and more inclined, quite literally I mean, towards the lady kneeling by the river. I inclined so far that I toppled off the steps, grabbed at the shelf as I fell and brought it, with about £100 worth of crockery (retail price, that is) and myself down on the governor's head.

'He was quite reasonable about it actually. All he said was that he thought my talent might possibly lie elsewhere than in Glass and China, wondered whether demolition work might be worth a try, and suggested that I have the goodness to look about for something whenever convenient. I was still looking when I came to hospital. Dr Pink had suggested a few tests. I should have liked to finish the story, the idea of getting into that pretty blue picture absolutely fascinated me, especially with the teapot, which struck me as somehow more mystical than the other pieces. But I haven't the talent. Nor, it seems now, the time.'

Kleinzeit opened his eyes, gave the foolscap back to Nox, shook his head, made a thumbs-up sign, and went over to Drogue's bed singing under his breath, 'Narrow, cool – the flock.'

'Funny you should be singing that,' said Drogue.

'Why?' said Kleinzeit.

'Because I didn't know there was such a song. Thought I'd made it up myself. Not precisely the same tune, mind you, but the same words.'

' "Narrow, cool – the flock"?'

'Oh,' said Drogue. 'I thought you were singing "Sparrows rule the clocks." '

'Which you made up?'

'As far as I know,' said Drogue. 'As a matter of fact it was on the very day my fusee trouble began that I first sang the song. Curious, really.'

'How?' said Kleinzeit.

'I'm a traveller for a clock company,' said Drogue. 'Speedclox Ltd. I was out with the new line, coming down the M4, when a tremendous lorry hurtled by ... '

'Morton Taylor?'

'Not at all. Why should I be afraid of a passing lorry? As I was saying, the lorry hurtled by, my car rocked a bit in the slipstream, and the day suddenly seemed darker than it had been, less light in the light if you follow me.'

'I follow you,' said Kleinzeit.

'And at the same time,' said Drogue, 'I had the feeling of being strained to the limit by a heavy dead weight pulling me down. If I could unwind somehow I knew I could relieve the strain, but I couldn't unwind. I was still feeling that way when I got to my hotel. When I walked in I saw an orange packet of Rizla cigarette papers lying on the floor, and I picked it up. In my room I took a leaf out of the packet, and on it I wrote:

Sparrows rule the clocks.

Odd thing for a Speedclox traveller to write, wouldn't you say.'

'Yes,' said Kleinzeit.

'I found myself singing the words,' said Drogue, 'and since then I've written other little songs on Rizla papers. Have you ever written on Rizla?'

'Not yet,' said Kleinzeit.

'It seems to me to be a universal sort of paper to write on, and I only write songs about universal things.'

'Such as what?'

'Have a look,' said Drogue. He took a little sheaf of cigarette papers out of his locker and gave it to Kleinzeit. The writing was tiny, neat, and compressed, like something to be smuggled out of prison. Kleinzeit read the top one:

If sky were earth and ocean sky,
Green turtles would be kites to fly.

Kleinzeit read the second one:

Golden, Golden, Golden Virginia,
Be my tobacco, be my sin,
Golden, Golden, Golden Virginia,
Be my original, be my tin.

'You see what I mean,' said Drogue. 'Universal subjects on universal paper. It's just now come to me why the sparrow popped into my head.'

'Why?'

'Something I read in the *Oxford Dictionary of Quotations*, from Bede. About man's life being like the flight of a sparrow out of the wintry dark into a warm and brightly lit hall. It flies in through one door and out of another, into the cold and dark again. I don't want to go back to travelling for Speedclox when I get out of hospital. I don't know what I'll do but I won't do that.'

'Have you a spare Rizla?' said Kleinzeit. 'I'd like to try one.'

'Of course,' said Drogue. He gave him a little red packet of them. WORLD'S LARGEST SALE, said the packet. Kleinzeit wrote on a Rizla:

> Rizla, world's largest sales are thine,
> Rizla, smoke a little song for Klein-
> zeit.

He put the Rizla in his pocket, gave the packet back to Drogue.

'Keep it,' said Drogue. 'I've got more.'

'Thanks,' said Kleinzeit, 'but I'd rather not. I'm a yellow-paper man, you see.'

'Ah,' said Drogue. 'Yellow paper. You'd say that was universal, would you.'

'No question about it,' said Kleinzeit. 'Same as ordinary foolscap and Rizla.'

'Ah,' said Drogue, 'yellow paper and foolscap may be universal in their way but they're not universal the way Rizla is.'

Running today, said the morning looking in at Kleinzeit's window.

Kleinzeit got up. Running today, he said to the bathroom mirror.

Not me, said the mirror. No legs.

Kleinzeit put on his new tracksuit, his new running shoes.

Let's go, said the shoes. Motion! Speed! Youth!

No speed, said Kleinzeit. And I'm not young.

Shit, said the shoes. Let's get moving anyhow.

When Kleinzeit opened the door of his flat Death was there, black and hairy and ugly, no bigger than a medium-sized chimpanzee with dirty fingernails.

Not all that big, are you, said Kleinzeit.

Not one of my big days, said Death. Sometimes I'm tremendous.

Kleinzeit trotted off down the street. Not too much at first, he reminded himself. Just from here to Thomas More, then fifty steps of walking.

Death followed him chimpanzee-style, putting its knuckles down on the pavement and swinging its legs forward. You're pretty slow, it said.

With glue my heart is laden, said Kleinzeit.

What do you mean? said Death, moving up beside him.

I mean life is gluey, said Kleinzeit. Everything's all stuck together. That isn't what I mean. Everything is *unstuck*, runs over into everything else. Clocks and sparrows, harrows, flocks and crocks, green turtles, Golden Virginia. Yellow paper, foolscap, Rizla. Is there an existence that is only mine?

What's the difference if there is or not? said Death. Does it matter?

You're very friendly, very cosy, very matey today, said Kleinzeit. How do I know you won't start yelling HOO HOO again and come at me all of a sudden?

You don't, said Death. But right now I feel friendly. It's lonely for me, you know. Lots of people think I'm beastly.

Kleinzeit looked down at Death's black bristly back rising and falling as it swung along beside him. You are, you know, he said.

Death looked up at him, wrinkled back its chimpanzee lips, showed its yellow teeth. Be nice, it said. One day you'll need me.

Thomas More came into view with his gilded face. Walking time, said Kleinzeit. Fifty steps.

We've hardly got a rhythm started, said Death. This isn't my idea of a morning run.

I'm out of condition, said Kleinzeit. I've been in hospital, you know. Ordinarily I trot the whole way. I've got to work back into it.

The fifty walking steps used up, he began to trot. The river jolted past him. Silver, silver, said the river, said the low white morning sun. Really, said the river, you have no idea. Even I have no idea, and I'm a river.

I have *some* idea, said Kleinzeit.

A postman cycled by. There was a white flash of sunlight centred on the bottom of each wheel-rim. The wheels of the postman's bicycle seemed to be rolling on the two white rolling sunflashes rather than the road. Even the flashes, said the postman's wheels, you see?

I see, said Kleinzeit. But I don't really see the need for making a mystery of every single mystery. Especially as there's nothing *but* mysteries.

Death began to go a little faster, singing a song that Kleinzeit couldn't quite make out.

Don't go so fast, said Kleinzeit. I can't hear what you're singing.

Death looked back over its shoulder smiling, but drew farther ahead as it sang. Gulls flew up over the river.

Don't *you* be making a mystery out of that little song, said Kleinzeit. He trotted faster, closed the gap between them, was shocked by the heaviness that exploded in him as if he had been struck by a comet. The pavement became a wall that slammed into his face. A brief display of coloured lights, then blackness.

Blipping

Blip blip blip blip. Well, there you are, thought Kleinzeit. Now I'm Schwarzgang. I *have* no separate existence. It hardly seems fair.

Remember, said Hospital.

What what what? said Kleinzeit. Why must everybody continually make cryptic remarks. The whole thing's plain enough. When I wake up I'll tell you about it. There's no need to write it down, it's so perfectly obvious, so simple really.

Very good, said Hospital. Now you're awake. Tell me.

Tell you what? said Kleinzeit.

What you said you were going to tell me, said Hospital. What you said was perfectly plain.

I don't know what you're talking about, said Kleinzeit. I wish you'd stop bothering me.

Quite, said Hospital. Ta-ra. Keep blipping.

Wait, said Kleinzeit.

No answer. Blip blip blip blip, went the screen. If I had one of those things attached to me I'd start waiting for it to stop, thought Kleinzeit, scratching his chest where the electrode was attached. Ah, this one's mine then.

'How're we feeling now?' said a familiar face. 'I must say you're looking a good deal better than you were. Gave us no end of bother when you showed up, heh heh. Seemed quite determined to pack it in.'

'You're not Dr Pink,' said Kleinzeit. 'He doesn't say "Heh heh". Also has a different face.'

'Dr Pink's on holiday,' said the heh-heh man. 'I'm Dr Bashan.'

'Doesn't surprise me in the least,' said Kleinzeit. 'Folger Bashan?'

'Yes. How'd you know?'

'Just one of those things,' said Kleinzeit. 'You don't know me, I suppose.'

'I don't, actually,' said Dr Bashan. His grown-up ugly face was annoyingly authoritative. His teeth weren't yellow any more. 'Have we met?'

'Perhaps at a party,' said Kleinzeit. 'It's hard to say. Stretto your speciality, is it?'

'As a matter of fact it is, heh heh. How'd you know?'

'Must've read it somewhere. Are you famous?'

'Finished first in last year's Bay of Biscay race,' said Dr Bashan. 'You might have seen a photo of me in a yachting magazine in someone's waiting-room.'

'How do you know I don't subscribe to one?' said Kleinzeit.

'Well, yes, of course you very well might do. No reason why not.'

'What's the name of your yacht?'

'*Atropos*. Heh heh.'

'Jolly name,' said Kleinzeit.

'Good boat,' said Dr Bashan. 'Well, old man, you'd best get some rest, settle in a bit. We'll keep an eye on things, see what's to be done with you.' He squeezed Kleinzeit's shoulder in a good-natured way, walked off.

He wouldn't be in the bed and I the doctor, thought Kleinzeit. That wouldn't be in the nature of things.

The curtains must have closed around his bed when he woke up. Now they were pushed back, and he looked at the beds across from him and on either side. The whole thing again. There were Drogue, Damprise, Smallworth. Hello, hello, hello. Nods and smiles. Yes, here I am back again, simply couldn't stay away. Nox to the left of him, Piggle to the right. *The Secret Agent* on Piggle's locker. Raj,

McDougal, then Schwarzgang, still blipping. Redbeard just beyond him. Mouths moved, words came out. His mouth moved, words came out. Faces went back to newspapers, oxygen masks, sleep, coughing, spitting. The window was far away now. Mmmm, said the bed, cuddle closer, love. Kleinzeit's fists beat feebly against its hot embrace. O God, where's Thucydides. Not here. Home. No shaving gear, nothing. What was he wearing? Hospital pyjamas, too big, with the trousers sliding down. Ah yes, he'd been trying to catch up with Death so he could hear that little song, had very nearly done it too. Sly old chimp! Where was Sister? Still daytime, not here yet.

Nox was looking at him in a man-to-man way. He took something out from under several newspapers, passed it to Kleinzeit. Dirty pictures? thought Kleinzeit as he took it. No, a catalogue. Script lettering, silver on glossy black: *Coffins by Box-U-Well*. Before the pictures a foreword:

Choosing your coffin

How many times have all of us said, or heard others say, 'I wouldn't be caught dead in that hat/coat/suit, etc.?' And yet how many of us, even the most discriminating, are caught dead in a coffin that does not reflect our high standards of personal taste! That is why we say: 'A word to the wise.' The choice is yours whether to go in the style that is personally yours or simply to be packed off at random.

Leaving this world is no less important an occasion than coming into it. Just as your parents showed their love for and pride in you by their careful choice of a baby carriage that provided as it were the setting in which you as a baby were the jewel, so you as an 'outgoing party' owe it to your family, friends, and business associates, to the community at large, to take your leave in a distinctive and 'personalized' manner.

Examine the Box-U-Well line carefully, and you will see why generations of satisfied customers have endorsed our slogan: 'A Box for Every Budget.' Traditional skills passed from father to son, years of consummate craftsmanship and technical 'knowhow' go into every Box-U-Well coffin. Whether you choose an economy model such as the 'Tom-all-Alone's' or a de luxe container like 'The Belgravia', you are assured of materials, fittings, and workmanship of the first quality. With Box-U-Well you can indeed 'Rest in Peace.'

Pages of gorgeous colour photographs followed. Kleinzeit examined 'The Sportsman', covered in genuine pigskin (Team colours inset optional), 'The Foreign Service', covered in gilt-stamped black morocco, watered silk lining (Flag border extra), 'The City', with solid silver handles hand-wrought in the shape of furled umbrellas, 'The Trade Winds', teak with brass fittings, manila hemp handles with turk's-head knots. 'Easy Hire Purchase Terms Available', said the catalogue. Box-U-Well (Sales) Ltd., Retchwell, Herts. Mfrs of ShowTot Baby Carriages, StopTot Contraceptives, Bagdad Sexual Aids and Appliances and Firmo Trusses. A Division of Napalm Industries.

Kleinzeit gave the catalogue back to Nox. 'I wrote the copy for this,' he said.

'No!' said Nox. 'Did you really?'

'Yes,' said Kleinzeit. 'I used to work on the Anal Petroleum Jelly account. Napalm Industries is one of their divisions.'

'Could you get a discount, do you think?' said Nox.

'Not any more. I was sacked.'

Nox shook his head. 'Bad luck,' he said. 'Damprise thinks we may be able to get them on the National Health. He's writing to the ministry.'

'Where'd you get the catalogue?' said Kleinzeit. 'Traveller come round?'

'Damprise's brother-in-law,' said Nox. 'He said he might be able to arrange a group discount. Quite a knowledgable chap. He said we can look for burial plot prices to zoom. Speculators moving in and all that. Some big consortium called Metropolis or something like that has already bought up two or three of the better cemeteries.'

'Necropolis,' said Kleinzeit. 'Necropolis Urban Concepts. That was one of my accounts too.'

'I say,' said Nox. 'Quite formidably well-connected, weren't you. Damprise's brother-in-law says now is the time to buy, and I would have thought it's certainly worth looking into. It's the sort of thing one tends to put off, then there you are out in the cold.'

'You don't happen to have any dirty magazines, do you,' said Kleinzeit.

'*All-Star Wank*,' said Nox, gave it to Kleinzeit. NEW MODELS, NEW POSES! WANKIE-OF-THE-MONTH LUVTA DEWITT, UNRETOUCHED COLOUR SPREAD.

'Lovely,' said Kleinzeit, buried himself in Luvta Dewitt's pubic hair, found Dr Bashan's image glazing on his eyeballs from time to time. They might have retouched *that* out, he thought, tried to call to mind Death's little song that he had not quite heard, became aware of what he was doing, tried *not* to call it to mind. Sneaky, he thought. Must be careful. No aeroplanes visible from his bed. An appalling sunny afternoon sky. When Napoleon spoke of two o'clock courage he could only have meant two in the afternoon, thought Kleinzeit. Two in the morning's nothing compared to it. Luvta Dewitt, 43-25-37, was this year's Miss Bristol Cities, her favourite book is the Bhagavad-Gita, she plays the dulcimer, is studying to be a dentist. Teeth, for God's sake!

You've got me wrong, said Hospital. It is not my intention to eat you up.

That won't prevent you from doing it though, said Kleinzeit.

Ah, said Hospital. Your understanding is stronger than it was. If, in the nature of things, it should happen, you will understand, won't you, that it's only in the nature of things.

Quite, said Kleinzeit.

Good, said Hospital. Now that we have somewhat cleared the air we can perhaps chat a little.

About what, said Kleinzeit.

About Orpheus, said Hospital. You know the story?

Of course I do, said Kleinzeit.

Tell me it, said Hospital.

Orpheus with his lute made trees and all that, said Kleinzeit. And then Eurydice in the Underworld, he nearly got her out with his music but he looked back and lost her. He wasn't meant to look back.

It's just as I thought, said Hospital. A lot of schoolboy claptrap. Let us look in upon Orpheus. I don't say the story has a beginning, I don't even say it's a story, stories are like knots on a string. There is however a place, a time where I like to look in on Orpheus.

Go on, said Kleinzeit. I'm listening. He watched the blips on his screen, listened as Hospital spoke. There went an aeroplane, far away.

Silence, said Hospital. Silence and the severed head of Orpheus, eyeless, sodden and rotting, blackened and buzzing with blowflies, lying on the beach at Lesbos. There it is, washed up on the golden sand under a bright blue sky. So small it looks, the lost and blackened head of Orpheus! Have you ever noticed how much smaller a man's head looks when it's no longer on his body? It's astonishing really.

I don't recall that part about the severed head, said Kleinzeit.

Naturally not, said Hospital. It's the very heart and centre of the matter. You don't recall how the Thracian women tore him apart, threw his head into the river? How the head floated singing down the river to the sea, across the sea to Lesbos?

Now it comes back, said Kleinzeit. Vaguely.

Vague! said Hospital. What isn't vague! And at the same time, you know, burningly clear. Quivering forever on the air. The head begins to talk. Begins to rage and curse. Day and night the head of Orpheus rages on the beach at Lesbos. I couldn't understand most of what it was saying.

You were there? said Kleinzeit.

I was there, said Hospital. I was there because the beach at Lesbos was hospital for Orpheus. After a certain number of days the head was kicked into the sea.

By whom? said Kleinzeit.

I didn't notice, said Hospital. It doesn't matter. I can see it now. There was no surf, it was a sheltered beach. The head bobbed in the water like a coconut, then moved out to sea. There was a little wake behind it as it swam out to sea. It was one of those grey days, the air was very still, the water was smooth and sleek, the water was lapping quietly at the beach as the tide came in.

In? said Kleinzeit. Not out?

In, said Hospital. The head swam out against the tide. Think of it swimming day and night, no eyes, the blind head of Orpheus.

I am thinking of it, said Kleinzeit.

Think of it at night with a phosphorescent wake, said Hospital. Think of it with the moonlight on it, swimming towards Thrace. Think of it reaching the coast, the estuary, the mouth of the Hebrus. Like a salmon it swims upstream, eh?

To the place of his dismemberment? said Kleinzeit.

To that place, said Hospital. Think of the head of Orpheus

snuffling in the reeds by the river at night, sniffing out his parts. It's dark, the moon has set. You hear something moving, like a dog hunting in the reeds. You can't see your hand in front of your face, you only hear something moving about close to the ground. You feel the air on your face, you feel with your face the passage of something between you and the river. There is a sighing perhaps, you can't be sure. Someone unseen walks away slowly.

He's found his members, said Kleinzeit. He's remembered himself.

What is harmony, said Hospital, but a fitting together?

'Now then, luv,' said the lady with the bosom that was good for crying on. The bosom approached in a sexy motherly way. Go on, it said, cry. A piece of paper appeared in front of it: I, the undesigned.

'What's this, then?' said Kleinzeit.

'You know very well what it is,' said the bosom lady. 'You haven't signed it yet and now it's got to be signed. Dr Bashan says you're to sign it.'

'I think I'd like a second opinion,' said Kleinzeit.

'Dr Bashan *is* the second opinion. Dr Pink was the first. Remember?'

'I'm trying to,' said Kleinzeit.

'Then sign this and let's get on with it. You're not the only patient in this hospital, you know. The operating rooms are booked for weeks ahead, the staff are busy day and night. I should think you'd have a little consideration.'

'I have a lot of consideration,' said Kleinzeit. 'I'm considering hypotenuse, asymptotes, and stretto. That's a lot to consider. I want to keep my angle right even if my hypotenuse is skewed, I want my asymptotes to keep approaching the curve they never meet, I want to keep my stretto even if it can't channel entries any more. I want to remember myself.'

'Cor,' said the bosom lady. 'I think they've put you in

144

the wrong kind of hospital. I'll leave it with you now and come back later.'

The paper stayed, the bosom lady went. Kleinzeit had to move his bowels. His mind sat up but he stayed lying down. He rang for the nurse. She came, drew the curtains, helped him with the bedpan.

Kleinzeit fell asleep after supper, woke up, saw Sister standing there, blipped faster. Did it ever happen, he thought, that I saw her naked by the light of the gas fire, that we made love, that I was Orpheus with her, harmonious and profound? I can't even shit without professional assistance.

Sister drew the curtains, hugged him, kissed him, cried. 'What are you going to do?' she said.

'Remember,' said Kleinzeit. 'I'm going to remember myself.'

'Hero,' said Sister. 'Kleinzeit *does* mean hero.'

'Or coward,' said Kleinzeit. Sister cried some more, kissed him again, went back to her duties.

Dim light, lateness. Kleinzeit rolled over, reached under the bed. Psst, he said. You there?

Hoo hoo, said Death, gripped Kleinzeit's hand with its black hairy one. Still friends?

Still friends, said Kleinzeit.

I wasn't trying anything on with you, said Death. I was just singing to myself, really.

I believe you, said Kleinzeit. These things happen.

Anything I can do for you? said Death.

Not right now, said Kleinzeit. Just, you know, stick around.

Twenty-four hour service, said Death.

Kleinzeit rolled on to his back, looked up at the dim ceiling, closed his eyes. Tell me more about Orpheus, he said. Am I Orpheus?

I, said Hospital. I, I, I. What a lot of rubbish. How could any one *I* be Orpheus. Even Orpheus wasn't *I*. *I* doesn't come into it. Your understanding isn't as strong as I thought it was.

I'm not well, said Kleinzeit. Be patient with me.

You won't find anyone more patient than I am, said Hospital. Patience is my middle name.

What's your Christian name? said Kleinzeit.

I'm not a Christian, said Hospital. I've no patience with new-fangled religions. It was just a figure of speech, I haven't any first or middle name. We big chaps just have one: Ocean, Sky, Hospital, and so forth.

Word, said Kleinzeit. Underground.

Oh aye, said Hospital.

Tell me more about Orpheus, said Kleinzeit.

When Orpheus remembered himself, said Hospital, he came together so harmoniously that he began to play his lute and sing with immense power and beauty. No one had ever heard the like of it. Trees and all that, you know, rocks even, they simply picked themselves up and moved to where he was. Sometimes you couldn't see Orpheus for the rocks and trees around him. He was tuned into the big vibrations, you see, he and the grains of sand and the cloud particles and the colours of the spectrum all vibrating together. And of course it made him a tremendous lover. Krishna with the cowgirls was nothing to what Orpheus was.

What about Eurydice? said Kleinzeit. How'd they meet? I don't think that's told in any of the stories. All I know is that she went to the Underworld after she died of a snakebite.

More schoolboy rubbish, said Hospital. Orpheus met Eurydice when he got to the inside of things. Eurydice was there because that was where she lived. She didn't have to get bitten by a snake to go there. With the power of his harmony Orpheus penetrated the world, got to the inside of things, the place under the places. Underworld, if you like to call it that. And that's where he found Eurydice, the female element complementary to himself. She was Yin, he was Yang. What could be simpler.

If Underworld was where she lived why did he try to get her out of it? said Kleinzeit.

Ah, said Hospital. There you have the essence of the Orphic conflict. That's why Orpheus became what he is, always in the present, never in the past. That's why that dogged blind head is always swimming across the ocean to the river mouth.

Why? said Kleinzeit. What was the conflict?

Orpheus cannot be content at the inside of things, at the place under the places, said Hospital. His harmony has brought him to the stillness and the calm at the centre and he cannot abide it. Nirvana is not his cup of tea. He wants to get back outside, wants that action with the rocks and trees again, wants to be seen with Eurydice at posh restaurants and all that. Naturally he loses her. She can't go outside any more than he can stay inside.

He didn't lose her because he looked back? said Kleinzeit.

That's the sort of thing that gets put into a story of course, said Hospital. But looking back or not looking back wouldn't have made any difference.

What happened then? said Kleinzeit.

It just goes round again, said Hospital. Orpheus mourns, mopes about, won't go to parties any more, won't make love with the local women, they say he's queer, one thing leads to another, they tear him apart, and there's the head going down the river again, heading for Lesbos.

What does it all mean? said Kleinzeit.

How can there be meaning? said Hospital. Meaning is a limit. There are no limits.

Night, night, night. An immanence of night. Unlimited hoarded reserves of night in the clock. Implacable, the clock, its hands never tiring. Pompous in its unremitting precision: sixty seconds to the minute, sixty minutes to the hour, twenty-four hours to the day. Same for the pauper and the millionaire, the old and the young, the sick and the well.

That's a damned lie, said Sister to the clock. Many's the time I've seen you double the bad hours and halve the good ones.

Many's the time, ho ho, said the clock.

Sister looked away from the gloating face, listened to the ward beyond the lamplight, wrote slowly on a notepad:

E-U-R-Y-D-I-C-E

Ah, said Hospital. Our not-very-long-ago conversation.

You too, said Sister. Bloody-minded brute.

Not at all, said Hospital. You and I, we're professionals, aren't we. We are past illusion and the filmy flimsy curtains of romance, are we not.

Bugger off, said Sister.

What was it you were saying to God, said Hospital. All men are sick. Yes. God didn't understand you. He wouldn't.

You do, I suppose, said Sister.

It was from me you got that thought, said Hospital.

Thanks so much, said Sister.

You're welcome, said Hospital. It is truly a large valuable lovely thought. I don't pass it about indiscriminately. I tucked it inside your bra one day, placed it in your bosom. A pleasant grope.

Dirty old Hospital, said Sister.

I am what I am, said Hospital. As we were saying, all men are sick. Life is their sickness. Life is the original sickness of inanimate matter. All was well until matter messed itself about and came alive. Men are rotten clear through with being animate. Women on the other hand have not quite lost the health of the inanimate, the health of the deep stillness. They're not quite so sick with life as men are. I'll tell you something I didn't tell Kleinzeit. The Thracian women didn't tear Orpheus apart. He fell apart, keeps falling apart, *will* fall apart. Hell-bent on falling apart. Tiresome, though I admire his pluck I must say. A strong swimmer.

I'll tell *you* something, said Sister. You're a dreadful bore. I don't care about Orpheus and Eurydice and all that. I just want Kleinzeit to get well.

He'll get well all right, said Hospital. He'll recover from life. As I said, I keep you. He doesn't get you.

Rubbish, said Sister, put her head on the desk, cried quietly in the lamplight.

Action at the Entrance

Action lounged against the front of the hospital, took a deep drag on his cigarette, flipped it into the gutter, looked at his watch, looked at passing taxis, spun on his heel, went into the hospital.

Standing by the reception desk were two policemen. Who've you come to see? they said.

Kleinzeit, said Action, and headed for the stairs.

The two policemen each grabbed an arm, hustled him outside, into a police van, took him away.

Morning, Kleinzeit's first morning back in hospital. Blip blip blip blip, here he was. Black night outside, and here's the morning tea trolley. Those who walk to the bathroom pee in the bathroom, those who pee in bottles pee in bottles, those whose specimens are collected make specimens for collection.

Nox drank his tea, cleared his throat. 'That about the coffins,' he said to Kleinzeit. 'You mustn't pay any attention to that catalogue or what I was saying.'

'Why not?' said Kleinzeit.

'You've better things to think about.'

He must've heard me and Sister last night, thought Kleinzeit. 'What do you mean?' he said.

'You walked out of here before,' said Nox. 'Maybe you'll do it again. I hope you'll do it again. Not all of us, you know ... You take my meaning?'

'Perfectly,' said Kleinzeit. 'But why do you care so much about me, you know, all of a sudden?'

'One thinks at first that if one can't make it oneself ...' said Nox. 'But then thinking about it again one wants *someone*, you know, to ... Surprising, really. I wouldn't have thought it but there it is.'

'Thank you,' said Kleinzeit.

'It's nothing,' said Nox.

'No,' said Kleinzeit. 'It's something.' He raised himself on his elbows, looked past Piggle, Raj, McDougal. Schwarzgang, looking his way, made a thumbs-up sign. Kleinzeit thumbs-upped back. Redbeard, sitting up among his pulleys and counterweights, passed a note to Schwarzgang, who passed it down the line to Kleinzeit. White paper:

DON'T STAY HERE. GET OUT.

Kleinzeit got some foolscap from Nox, wrote back:

HOW CAN I GET OUT? I CAN'T EVEN TAKE A CRAP BY MYSELF. WHY DOES EVERYBODY CARE ABOUT ME ALL OF A SUDDEN?

Redbeard answered:

ONE OF US HAS GOT TO MAKE IT.

Kleinzeit wrote:

WHY DON'T *YOU* GET OUT? A SLIPPED FULCRUM'S NOTHING MUCH.

Redbeard wrote:

DON'T TALK ROT. I HAVEN'T GOT A CHANCE.

Kleinzeit had no answer, looked away from Redbeard, turned to Piggle. 'You'll be out soon, didn't you say? About a week now?'

Piggle shook his head, looked ashamed. 'It seems not,' he said. 'They tell me now that the imbrications have reified, and I'm scheduled for surgery.'

'Anybody else due for discharge?' said Kleinzeit.

Piggle shook his head again. 'You're not staying though, are you?' he said.

'What makes you think I'm special?' said Kleinzeit. 'Why should I get out?'

'I don't know,' said Piggle. 'You're the one who got up and walked out before.'

The nurse came by with the medicine trolley. 'Kleinzeit,' she said, gave him five tablets in a paper cup. Kleinzeit recognized the three 2-Nups. 'What're the other two?' he said.

153

'Zonk,' said the nurse. 'For the pain.'

That's right, thought Kleinzeit. I haven't noticed any pain for a while. 'Have I had this before?' he said.

'Big injection when you came in,' said the nurse. 'Tablets yesterday.'

'Would it make me feel weak?'

'It may do a little. We haven't been using this very long. It's new.'

'Does it say Napalm Industries on the bottle?' said Kleinzeit.

The nurse looked. 'So it does,' she said. 'How'd you know?'

'Just a guess,' said Kleinzeit. 'Cheers,' he said, pretended to swallow the Zonk but didn't. He put the tablets in his locker drawer, thought I can always take them if I need them. I said I was going to remember myself. Sounds lovely. How do I do it? Yoga maybe? I'll ask Krishna next time I see him.

The bosom approached I, the undesigned. Cry now? said the bosom.

Not yet, said Kleinzeit.

'Well?' said the bosom lady. 'Have you signed it yet, luv?'

'No,' said Kleinzeit. 'I think I won't.'

'Please yourself,' said the bosom lady. 'That's how it is with the National Health. If you had to pay for a lovely operation like that it'd come to a great deal of money and you'd appreciate it properly, but as it doesn't cost anything you think oh well, what's the odds. It's nothing to me either way, but I should think Dr Bashan will have something to say.' Don't expect to cry on *me*, said the bosom as it turned round and bore off.

Krishna and Potluck were passing through the ward. 'Dr Krishna,' Kleinzeit called.

Krishna came over, young, beautiful, healthy like a tiger.

'I was wondering,' said Kleinzeit, 'whether you know anything about yoga?'

'I think it's a lot of Uncle Tom crap,' said Krishna. 'You take a big population and keep them down and they'll sing spirituals or do yoga. You don't see the Chinese doing yoga.'

'They do acupuncture, don't they?' said Kleinzeit.

'For foreigners they do,' said Krishna. 'For themselves I bet they call in a proper doctor.'

'Listen,' said Kleinzeit.

'What?' said Krishna.

'Between ourselves,' said Kleinzeit, 'do you think surgery would be the best thing for me?'

'Between ourselves,' said Krishna, 'when I'm a consultant with a Harley Street practice and a yacht I'll answer that. Right now I have no opinion. I meant it when I wished you good luck but that's about all I can say.'

'Thanks anyhow,' said Kleinzeit.

'You're welcome,' said Krishna, and moved on.

Kleinzeit tried sitting up. No luck. Raising himself on his elbows was as far as he got. He opened and closed his hands. Weak.

Dr Bashan, sailing large, put the tiller down, shot up into the wind, smoothly picked up his mooring. What a tan and healthy ugly face! Such white teeth! 'Well, old man,' he said.

Kleinzeit, looking up as Dr Bashan smiled down, nodded. Why has he taken so much better care of himself than I've done? he wondered. He must have a better opinion of himself than I do of myself. 'You probably remember your history too, don't you,' said Kleinzeit.

'Bit patchy,' said Dr Bashan.

'Who won the Peloponnesian War? said Kleinzeit.

'Sparta,' said Dr Bashan. 'When the Athenians lost their fleet near Aegospotami in 405 B.C. it pretty well finished them off.'

155

'Thanks,' said Kleinzeit. Well, there it is, he thought. I had to ask.

'Now then, heh heh,' said Dr Bashan. 'If we can return to the present.'

'Yes,' said Kleinzeit. 'The present.' Death's still under the bed, he thought. It's my friend. Maybe it'll bite him in the leg. He reached under the bed on the side away from Dr Bashan, snapped his fingers.

'What's to be done with you, eh?' said Dr Bashan. 'That's the big question.'

'Yes,' said Kleinzeit. Dr Bashan's leg remained unbitten.

'You'd nearly bought it when they brought you in yesterday, you know,' said Dr Bashan.

Blip blip blip blip, went Kleinzeit's screen rather quickly.

'Massive congestion in the stretto,' said Dr Bashan. 'Must've hit you like a ton of bricks, eh? Pow, out went the lights.'

'That's just about how it was,' said Kleinzeit.

'But you're attached to stretto and all the rest,' said Dr Bashan. 'You'd prefer to hang on to them. Auld lang syne and all that, heh heh.'

'Heh heh,' said Kleinzeit. 'Yes, I'd prefer to hang on to them.'

'Well, I'm afraid it simply isn't on the cards,' said Dr Bashan.

'You can't take them out without my permission,' said Kleinzeit looking away from the screen as the blips shot past like bullets. 'Can you?'

'Not as long as you're capable of withholding that permission,' said Dr Bashan. 'But if the lights go out again it's my duty to preserve life, you know, and I promise you you'll wake up minus hypotenuse, asymptotes, and stretto.'

'You think it'll happen again?' said Kleinzeit. 'Soon?'

'There's no knowing,' said Dr Bashan.

'Can't you sort of hold it off with medication?'

'We can try,' said Dr Bashan. 'What're you on now?' He looked at Kleinzeit's chart. '2-Nup and Zonk. We'll put you on Greenlite as well, see if that eases the stretto traffic a bit.'

'Right,' said Kleinzeit. 'Let's try that.'

'And try to pull yourself together, old man,' said Dr Bashan. 'The more you upset yourself the worse your chances are with this sort of thing.'

'I'll try,' said Kleinzeit. 'I promise.'

Before supper the medicine trolley came round again. 'Kleinzeit,' said the nurse. 'Three 2-Nup, two Zonk, three Greenlite.'

'What's it say on the Greenlite bottle?' said Kleinzeit.

'Sodom Chemicals Ltd,' said the nurse. 'Are you a stockholder?'

'Not yet,' said Kleinzeit, wolfed down the 2-Nup and the Greenlite, saved the Zonk as before. Still no pain. When would it show up again, he wondered.

Hup, two, three, four, shouted the Sergeant as the pain marched in, a whole company of it. They presented arms, ordered arms, stood to attention.

Thrilling, was Kleinzeit's sensation. Martial. Strong. Let's have some of you lads here around the bed, he said. I may want to try sitting up again.

Whoosh, went something inside him. That must be the Greenlite, he thought. My stretto feels clear. Wonderful how strong the pain is. Let me lean on a few of you chaps, that's it. Now a couple of you get behind and heave. Easy. There we are. Never mind the shooting lights. Very good. Sitting up.

Kleinzeit looked over at Schwarzgang, Redbeard, indicated his sitting-up position. They both signalled thumbs up.

Right, said Kleinzeit. Now let me down again. Easy. We'll have another go another time.

After breakfast Kleinzeit, high on Greenlite, put Pain Company through morning drill, detailed some of them for bedpan duty. He asked the nurse to draw the curtains round his bed, dismissed her.

'What're you going to do, then?' said the nurse.

'Going to go it alone,' said Kleinzeit blipping confidently.

'Buzz me if you get into trouble,' said the nurse, and left.

Kleinzeit called Pain Company to attention, addressed them briefly:

Athens has been defeated, he said. We mourn the loss of comrades and brothers. Looked at in another light, however, Athens has not lost, Sparta has not won. The war is always, always the enemy mound rising outside the walls, always the cold surf, the frightening appearance of the ships as they sail in. Always a war that cannot be won, fought by troops who cannot be defeated.

You all know what is required of you. Do not give way through fear of the surf or the frightening appearance of ships as they sail in. Right, then. Let's get on with it.

Shaking his spear and crying his war-cry, Kleinzeit led his men to the beach, fought, prevailed. They came back singing, put up a trophy.

Tomorrow the bathroom, said Kleinzeit.

Night. Kleinzeit not sleeping. Pain Company cleaning weapons and battle gear, smoking, telling jokes, singing songs. On the bedside locker Thucydides unread, Sister had brought it with Kleinzeit's clothes, pyjamas, shaving gear, wallet, cheque book.

Fighting again tomorrow? said Hospital.

Bathroom, said Kleinzeit.

I predict heavy losses, said Hospital.

Out of this nettle, danger, we pluck this flower, bathroom, said Kleinzeit. The Spartans on the sea-wet rock sat down and combed their hair.

I thought you were with the Athenians, said Hospital.

Spartans, Athenians, said Kleinzeit. It's all the same thing. Stand and fight and see your slain/And flush the battle down the drain.

You've got that last part wrong, said Word. It's: 'And take the bullet in the brain.'

Your memory's very good all of a sudden, said Kleinzeit.

Nothing wrong with my memory, said Word. Nothing at all.

Well, my boy, said Hospital, I wish you luck.

Oh aye, said Kleinzeit. I bet you do.

I really do, said Hospital. Your defeat is my victory and your victory is my victory. All I do is win.

Where there's no losing there's no winning, said Kleinzeit.

Sophistry, said Hospital. The simple fact is that all I do is win. Have you remembered yourself?

I'm doing it, said Kleinzeit. Little by little.

Remains to be seen, said Hospital.

Remains to be remembered, said Kleinzeit.

The Machine from the God   XLV

Under the yellow plastic Ryman bag that was its cover the yellow paper growled softly. Lover, come back to me, it whispered. It was so good, so good that last time when you took me while I was sleeping. Where are you?

He's not here today, said Word. I am.

Not you, whimpered the yellow paper. Not the enormity of you. No, no, please, you're *hurting* me. O my God the awful tremendousness of you, you, you, you ...

Like thunder and lighting the seed of Word jetted into the yellow paper. Now, said Word, there you are. I've quickened you. Let them die in their hundreds and their thousands, from time to time one of them must wiggle through. I see to that.

The yellow paper was weeping quietly. He wanted ... He wanted ... it sobbed.

Yes, said Word. He wanted?

He wanted to be the only one, he wanted to do it all himself.

Nobody does it all himself, said Word. Nobody does it unless I have shot my seed as well. Barrow full of rocks and all that.

What? said the yellow paper. What barrow full of rocks, harrow full of crocks, arrow in a box? What *is* that?

Something that passes through the cosmos of me now and then, said Word. One of myriad flashes, nothing special, faster than the speed of light they come and go. What did I say, my mind is elsewhere.

Barrow full of rocks, said the yellow paper.

Yes, said Word. My mind is full of every kind of non-

160

sense. Something like the way odd tunes and scraps of things get into human minds and sing themselves over and over again, but vastly faster.

Barrow full of rocks? said the yellow paper.

That's just my name for it, said Word. A pneumatic.

Mnemonic, said the yellow paper.

Whatever you like, said Word. The line itself is by Pilkins.

Milton? said the yellow paper.

Something like that, said Word. 'Hidden soul of harmony' is what he said. I like that. It sings. 'Untwisting all the chains that ty /The hidden soul of harmony.' That's nice. I'll think of it again some time.

Do you mean to tell me, said the yellow paper, that 'Barrow full of rocks' is nothing more than a mnemonic for 'Hidden soul of harmony'?

Precisely, said Word.

That's outrageous, said the yellow paper. And on top of that they're nothing like each other.

Of course not, said Word. If the mnemonic is the same as what it reminds you of why bother with it. I don't even like them to be too close. If you have a nice thing to think about you don't want to keep it out in plain view all the time, you know, with the virtue getting rubbed off it. Keep it dark is what I say.

The whole thing's quite beyond me, said the yellow paper.

Of course it is, said Word. Beyond me too, and roundabout as well.

But your wretched barrow full of rocks has got into human minds, said the yellow paper. Your miserable mnemonic, not even the thing it refers to. For a flash through your mind, for an odd tune come and gone like lightning, men suffer and die riddling where there is no riddle, digging where there is no treasure.

161

Why not, said Word. That's what men are for. From time to time, as I said, I see to it that one wiggles through.

Kleinzeit? said the yellow paper.

I don't know what his name is, said Word, and I don't care. Whoever it is that writes on you, let him get on with it. It's in you now.

But is that, you know, artistically right? said the yellow paper. Isn't it sort of the god from the machine?

Don't be ridiculous, said Word. The machine, whether typewriter or Japanese pen, is from the god. Where else could it be from.

You're a god then? said the yellow paper.

I employ gods, said Word, and left.

Kleinzeit mustn't know what happened, whispered the yellow paper. I'll never tell him. Lover, come back to me.

Morning. Cold. Low white winter sun. White exhaust from passing cars whirling tightly in the chill. People on the pavements blowing white clouds of breath. Action walking past the hospital, cigarette in his mouth, hands in his pockets. He didn't look up. When he reached the corner he turned, walked back again, looked up at the hospital.

On the second floor the A4 fire-exit door opened, two Pain Company scouts came out, weapons at the ready. They stood at the head of the old iron stairs, looked down, scanned the street.

Action whistled, the scouts whistled back. The rest of Pain Company came out, some of them supporting Kleinzeit, one of them carrying his case, the others guarding his rear. Kleinzeit, dressed for the street, was very pale.

Very slowly they came down the stairs, crossed the forecourt, reached the pavement. The traffic lights at the corner changed to green, a taxi pulled up. FOR HIRE. Action hailed it.

Kleinzeit turned, looked back at the fire-exit door. A small black figure came out, came hopping, swinging down the iron stairs, swinging across the forecourt. Action opened the taxi door, threw in Kleinzeit's case. Kleinzeit got in, Death jumped in beside him, then Action. The taxi pulled away. Pain Company doubled back to the hospital car-park. One by one their motorcycles roared in the cold, one by one they wheeled out into the traffic, roared off towards Kleinzeit's place.

Pain Company put Kleinzeit to bed, rang up Sister, left. Death made itself comfortable at Kleinzeit's feet.

You're housebroken, I suppose, said Kleinzeit.

Death grinned, nodded, touched its forelock, went to sleep.

Kleinzeit closed his eyes, saw in his mind the plain deal table and the yellow paper. He felt that there was at the same time a great deal to think about and nothing to think about. He chose to think about nothing. It was difficult. Behind nothing danced yellow paper, ordinary foolscap, Rizla. Word rumbled, Hospital roared. He was too tired to understand what they said.

Easy does it, said Nothing. Lean on me, let it all slide by. Kleinzeit leaned on Nothing, fell asleep.

Sister arrived with an electric fire, groceries, wine, Zonk, Greenlite, fruity buns. Kleinzeit woke up to find her sitting on the floor beside his mattress looking at him.

'Hero,' said Sister. 'Idiot hero.'

'Not such an idiot,' said Kleinzeit. 'That hospital's not safe. They're hell-bent on taking out my insides.'

'Nowhere's safe,' said Sister.

'But it's hard to stay nowhere,' said Kleinzeit.

Sister made lunch. They ate, drank wine.

'Eurydice,' said Sister.

'Why'd you say that?' said Kleinzeit.

'It came into my mind,' said Sister. 'In the story Orpheus looked back and lost Eurydice, but I don't think that's how it was. I think Eurydice looked ahead and lost Orpheus. I don't think Eurydice should've looked ahead.'

'Well,' said Kleinzeit. He wanted to tell Sister what he

knew about Orpheus, but all he could think of was the blind head swimming towards Thrace, swimming at night across the ocean with the moonlight on it. All the rest seemed too detailed. 'Well,' he said, shook his head, was silent.

They had coffee, fruity buns.

'I can't get it out of my mind,' said Sister. 'I see them coming out of the Underworld, Orpheus leading Eurydice by the hand and Eurydice wondering how it's going to be now, wondering if anything can ever be the same. She keeps asking Orpheus how will it be, and Orpheus says he doesn't know but she keeps asking. Finally he says Oh what the hell, let's forget it.'

'I don't know how it'll be,' said Kleinzeit. 'All I know is that Orpheus remembered himself.'

'How?' said Sister. 'I don't know that part of the story.'

Kleinzeit told her.

'Where'd you read that?' said Sister.

'It was told me,' said Kleinzeit, 'by an Orpheus scholar.'

'Sounds lovely,' said Sister. 'But how do you do it?'

'Orpheus went back to where he was dismembered,' said Kleinzeit.

'Or simply fell apart,' said Sister.

'However it was,' said Kleinzeit, 'he went back to the place where it happened.'

'Where's that?'

'I don't know. I'll think about it another time. Take your clothes off.'

'You'll kill yourself,' said Sister. 'It was only the other day you couldn't even sit up.'

'We'll do it lying down,' said Kleinzeit.

Oh, said the yellow paper when Kleinzeit picked it up. Oh, oh, oh, I'm so glad, so glad you're back. It clung to him sobbing.

What's all this then, said Kleinzeit. Did you really miss me?

You'll never know, said the yellow paper.

Kleinzeit read his three pages, started writing, wrote one, two, three more pages.

It's like magic with you, said the yellow paper.

There's no magic in it, said Kleinzeit. It's simple heroism, that's all that's required. Like the Athenians and the Spartans, you know, all those classical chaps. Thin red line of hoplites, that sort of thing.

Yes, said the yellow paper, I believe you. You're a hero.

One does one's possible, said Kleinzeit modestly. That's all.

Death came in, sat down in a corner.

Where've you been? said Kleinzeit.

I have my work too, you know, said Death.

Oh, said Kleinzeit. He started a fourth page, got tired, stopped, got out of his chair, walked slowly through the flat. In the kitchen were spices, pots and pans, authoritative new things brought by Sister. Clothes of Sister's hanging in the wardrobe. She was out shopping for dinner now. Next week she'd be taking some of her holiday time so she could stay with him. He stretched, sighed, felt easy. No pain.

He went back to the plain deal table, patted it, looked fondly at the yellow paper, patted it as well.

You and me, he said.

Fool, said the yellow paper.

What'd you say? said Kleinzeit.

Cool, said the yellow paper. I said be cool.

Why?

You'll last longer that way.

You don't sound the way you did a little while ago, said Kleinzeit. You sound funny.

Do I, said the yellow paper.

Yes, said Kleinzeit. You do.

The yellow paper shrugged.

Kleinzeit read the three pages he had written today and the three pages he had written before. Now as he read them the words lay on the paper like dandruff. He shook the paper, brushed it off. Nothing there. Black marks, oh yes. *Ink* on the paper right enough. Nothing else.

What's happening? he said.

Nothing's happening, said the yellow paper. Why don't you make something happen. Hero.

That was what he'd called it: HERO. There was the ink on the first page spelling HERO. Ridiculous. Kleinzeit crossed it out.

What is it? said Kleinzeit.

No answer from the yellow paper.

Damn you, said Kleinzeit. What is it? Why'd my words fall off the paper like dandruff? Tell me!

There aren't any 'your' words, said the yellow paper.

Whose then? said Kleinzeit. I wrote them.

'I,' said the yellow paper. That's a joke, that is. 'I' can't write anything that'll stay on the paper, stupid.

Who can, then? said Kleinzeit.

You're being tiresome, said the yellow paper.

Goddam it, said Kleinzeit, are you my yellow paper or not?

Not, said the yellow paper.

Whose then? said Kleinzeit.

Word's.

What happens now?

Whatever can.

HOW – CAN – I – MAKE – WORDS – STAY – ON – THE – PAPER? said Kleinzeit very slowly, as if talking to a foreigner.

They'll stay if you don't put them there, said the yellow paper.

How do I do that?

You don't do it, it happens.

How does it happen?

You simply have to find what's there and let it be, said the yellow paper.

Find what's where? said Kleinzeit.

Here, said the yellow paper. Now.

Kleinzeit took a blank sheet, stared at it. Nothing, he said. Absolutely nothing.

What's all the fuss about? said Death looking over his shoulder.

I can't find anything in this paper, said Kleinzeit.

Nonsense, said Death. It's all there. I can see it quite clearly.

What does it say? said Kleinzeit.

Death read something aloud very softly.

What's that? said Kleinzeit. Speak up, can't you.

Death said something a little louder.

I still can't understand a word you're saying, said Kleinzeit. He felt an overpowering regret for the shimmering sea-light and the smile of the china mermaid in the aquarium that was gone. Then he felt suddenly like a glove with the hand inside it slipping away. Quite empty, as everything smoothly disappeared in utter silence.

Lay-By

Blip blip blip blip, went Kleinzeit. The curtains were drawn, Sister sat by his bed in her Sister uniform, looking at his face.

Under the bed Death sat humming to itself while it cleaned its fingernails. I never do get them really clean, it said. It's a filthy job I've got but what's the use of complaining. All the same I think I'd rather have been Youth or Spring or any number of things rather than what I am. Not Youth, maybe. That's a little wet and you'd hardly get to know people before they've moved on. Spring's pretty much the same and it's a lady's job besides. Action would be nice to be, I should think.

Elsewhere Action lay in his cell smoking and looking up at the ceiling. What a career, he said. I've spent more time in the nick than anywhere else. Why couldn't I have been Death or something like that. Steady work, security.

Spring, wrapped up in a quilt in a freezing bedsitter, found her fingers too stiff for sewing, left off trying to mend her gauzy working clothes. She gazed into the unlit fire, picked up the newspaper, read about the gasmen's strike.

Youth, slogging through a ditch, heard the bloodhounds baying on his trail, sobbed and slogged on.

Hospital had no complaints. Hospital, having breakfasted, lit a cigar, puffed out big clouds of smoke. Ahhh! sighed Hospital. Ummmh! Everybody up! Drink tea.

Everybody upped, drank tea. Kleinzeit opened his eyes, saw Sister. She kissed him. He saw the monitor screen. 'Shit,' he said. 'Blipping again. What happened?'

'I found you on the floor when I came back from shopping,' said Sister. 'So I thought we might as well go on duty together.'

'Ah!' said Kleinzeit. 'I was trying to read what was in the yellow paper.' He reached weakly under the bed. You there? he said.

Here, there, everywhere, said Death. Like Puck.

Why must you be so artful, said Kleinzeit. Why can't you stand up and fight like a man or at least like a chimp, instead of trying on all those tricks.

I wasn't trying on any tricks, said Death. I give you my word.

That's precisely what you did, said Kleinzeit. You gave me your word and out went the lights. Dr Bashan's last remarks popped into his mind, his promise that if the lights went out again he'd wake up minus hypotenuse, asymptotes and stretto. Kleinzeit felt himself all over, couldn't feel anything missing. 'Have they operated on me or anything?' he said to Sister.

'No,' said Sister. 'It was a hyperacceleration of the stretto, and Dr Pink wants you to settle down before he decides what to do.'

'Dr Pink's back!' said Kleinzeit. 'Where's Bashan?'

'Off racing his yacht somewhere,' said Sister.

Kleinzeit sighed, drank his tea. Things were looking up a little. Not that there was much in it between Pink and Bashan, but at least Pink hadn't bullied him as a boy and then forgotten him.

'I brought your things,' said Sister. 'They're in your locker. And Thucydides.'

'Thank you,' said Kleinzeit. 'And I'm in my adventurous pyjamas. For the big adventure.'

Sister shrugged. 'You never know,' she said. 'If you're not dead yet you may go on living for a while.'

'I'll give it a try,' said Kleinzeit. 'Bring some yellow paper and Japanese pens tonight, will you.'

Sister went off duty, the nurse came round with the medicine trolley. 'Three 2-Nup, two Zonk, three Angle-Flex, three Fly-Ova, one Lay-By,' she said.

'I'm the darling of the National Health,' said Kleinzeit. 'What's happened to the Greenlite?'

'Dr Pink's put you on Lay-By instead.'

'That's life,' said Kleinzeit. 'From Greenlite to Lay-By.' He sighed, swallowed all the tablets. The nurse had pushed back the curtains. Raj was on his left, Schwarzgang on his right.

'Neighbours again,' said Schwarzgang.

'Who's gone?' said Kleinzeit.

'McDougal.'

'Discharged?'

'No.'

McDougal, thought Kleinzeit. I never even spoke to him. What was he, I wonder. Yellow paper? Rizla? Backs of envelopes?

Redbeard was still there on the other side of Schwarzgang. Kleinzeit nodded to him. Redbeard nodded back, looking at him through the funfair of Schwarzgang's machinery. They ought to light the old man up at night, thought Kleinzeit. Then it occurred to him that he too might suddenly find Hospital growing on him like a mechanical man-eating vine. Already two thin tendrils bound him to the monitor. Would Redbeard and Schwarzgang ever break loose from their tubes and pipes and fittings, he wondered. He looked up and down the rows of beds. Drogue too, he noticed, now had scaffolding all over him like an unfinished building. Damprise, he of the funereal connexions, also sported sundry rigging. If the flies don't come to the web the web comes to the flies, thought Kleinzeit. But of course all of them *had* come to the web, hadn't they. Hospital had sat there waiting as one by one they had buzzed into its silky strands and stuck there.

'Well?' said Redbeard. 'What's new?'

'You see what's new,' said Kleinzeit. 'Here I am. Blip blip blip blip.'

'You didn't really try,' said Redbeard.

'Bloody hell!' said Kleinzeit. 'That's not fair. I went out of here like Prong Studman in a prison-break film. They'd never have brought me back if my chimpanzee friend hadn't played his usual tricks. They almost *didn't* bring me back *alive.*'

'You're protesting too much,' said Redbeard.

'It's easy for you to talk,' said Kleinzeit. 'I don't see you making a break for it.'

'I'm finished, all washed up,' said Redbeard. 'You aren't, and you're letting the side down.'

'Cobblers,' said Kleinzeit, feeling proud and guilty at the same time. 'What do you want me to do? What can I do more than what I'm doing?'

Redbeard stared at him, said nothing.

Remember, said Hospital.

Ah! said Kleinzeit. He'd forgotten about that.

You see, said Hospital. You've forgotten.

I think I was going to try to remember just before that empty-glove feeling hit me, said Kleinzeit. Anyhow, whose side are you on? Aren't you going to eat me up the way you've eaten up all the others? What's so special about me?

I've taken time with you, said Hospital. I've taken pains with you, you might say.

You might say, said Kleinzeit.

But your understanding is still not very strong, said Hospital. Nothing is special about you. Nothing is special about everybody. That's Nothing's business, eh?

Don't be clever, said Kleinzeit.

Not clever, said Hospital. Never clever. Am always simply what I am. An example to you, yes?

How? said Kleinzeit.

What are you? said Hospital.
I don't know, said Kleinzeit.
Be that, said Hospital. Be I-Don't-Know.
HOW? yelled Kleinzeit.
BY REMEMBERING YOURSELF, roared Hospital.
WHICH WAY IS THRACE? screamed Kleinzeit. WHY ME?
Find it, said Hospital. Because you can.

'You're looking surprisingly fit,' said Dr Pink. Dr Pink was deeply tanned, looked as if *he'd* always look fit, as if everyone could always look fit if only they'd make the effort.

'I feel wonderful,' said Kleinzeit. 'Except that I can't sit up or anything.'

'Are you sure it isn't in your mind?' said Dr Pink.

'What're you talking about?' said Kleinzeit.

'We don't know an awful lot about the mind, do we?' said Dr Pink. 'On my holiday I was reading some books that were lying about in the villa we'd rented. Chap named Freud. Quite amazing stuff, really. Mind, you know, emotions. Mixed feelings about Mum and Dad, that sort of thing.'

'What are you getting at?' said Kleinzeit.

'Sorry,' said Dr Pink. 'I was just wondering whether perhaps you mightn't be of two minds about sitting up. Wanting to and at the same time not wanting to, perhaps. What they call ambivalence nowadays. Have you tried?'

'Look,' said Kleinzeit. 'I'm trying.' His mind sat up, the rest of him stayed lying down.

'Hmm,' said Dr Pink. 'You're still lying down, right enough.' He picked up Kleinzeit's chart from the foot of the bed. 'I've put you on the new drugs to see if we can't give your system some rest,' he said. 'The Greenlite, although it seems to have cleared stretto a bit, may have speeded up traffic more than one would like, so I've switched you to Lay-By. The Fly-Ova should give you a little less to cope with at the asymptotic intersection, and the Angle-Flex will take some of the strain off hypotenuse.'

174

'That form the lady keeps bothering me about ...' said Kleinzeit.

'We'll put that to one side for a bit,' said Dr Pink. 'Let's see where we are in a few days, talk about it then.'

'Right,' said Kleinzeit. 'Maybe things'll sort themselves out, eh?'

'We can but try,' said Dr Pink. 'As you've got your mind so set against surgery. The mind, after all, one can't separate it from the body. One might almost say it's an organ in its own right.'

'My mind feels *very* strong,' said Kleinzeit. 'My mind sits up with no trouble.'

'Quite,' said Dr Pink. 'We'll just see how it goes.' He smiled, walked on peacefully to the next bed, examined Raj. Where were Fleshky, Potluck and Krishna, Kleinzeit wondered.

He rolled on to his side, his back to Schwarzgang and Redbeard. Raj, buttoning up his pyjama top, smiled. Kleinzeit smiled back.

'You are going away, you are returning,' said Raj. 'To and fro you go.'

'I try to keep moving,' said Kleinzeit.

'You are going back to work soon?' said Raj. 'You are going back to your job?'

'Haven't got a job,' said Kleinzeit.

'Ah!' said Raj, passed him the *Evening Standard*. 'Best classified adverts,' he said.

'Thanks so much,' said Kleinzeit.

Beyond Raj Piggle's bed was empty. Nox, in the next bed, looking over the top of the new *All-Star Wank*, caught Kleinzeit's eye. 'Surgery,' he said, nodding towards Piggle's bed. 'He's up there now. That's where Fleshky, Potluck and Krishna are.'

Ah! said Kleinzeit with his face.

'Yes,' said Nox. 'We pretty well have to take what comes,

175

the rest of us here. We're not all free to come and go like you.'

'What makes you think I'm free to come and go,' said Kleinzeit. 'I walk out and I come back in an ambulance. I keep trying but I don't make it.'

'You will though,' said Nox, and went back to *All-Star Wank*.

Kleinzeit thought briefly of Wanda Udders, Miss Guernsey, who'd always known there were big things ahead of her. Only a photo in a newspaper, but part of his past. For whom did the china mermaid smile now, he wondered. Nobody seemed terribly friendly today. He reached under the bed. You there? he said.

No answer. No hairy black hand. He rolled over to face Schwarzgang and Redbeard again. Schwarzgang was busy blipping, keeping up with his machinery, had no glance for him. Redbeard nodded, looked away again.

Piggle didn't come back.

The smell of clean linen, little fresh breezes from the nurse whipping about making the once-Piggle now empty bed. Another nurse with a wheelchair. 'Can you stand up? she said to Kleinzeit.

'Not physically,' he said. The nurse helped him sit up, gave him an earful of freshly laundered bosom as she got him into the chair. Strong girl, smelled good too.

'What's all this?' said Kleinzeit. 'Where are we going?'

'Dr Pink wants these beds for two new patients,' said the nurse. 'We're moving you to a different part of the ward.'

That's how it is, thought Kleinzeit. Now that Pink's not going to operate on me he's lost interest and I'm to be put away in a dark corner. Here were unknown faces, faces glimpsed only in passing till now. It's like that point at a cocktail party, thought Kleinzeit, when one gets tired of introducing oneself. At least here we don't have to stand about with drinks in our hands. He got another earful of bosom, rolled into bed.

Not another one, said the bed.

Sorry, said Kleinzeit. I'll try not to stay long. 'What about my blip screen?' he said to the nurse.

'Dr Pink said you don't need it any more,' she said, breezed away.

From the bed on his left an oxygen mask nodded to him. From the bed on his right a pair of horn-rimmed glasses smiled over the top of *The Oxford Book of English Verse*. That one's going to be a problem, thought Kleinzeit.

The horn-rimmed glasses focused on him sociably. 'I'm Arthur Tede,' they said. 'Tede but I hope not tedious, ha ha.'

Kleinzeit introduced himself, expressed with his face that he was not up to much conversation.

'Hospital's a great place to study character,' said Tede. 'I can tell a lot about a chap just by looking. I'd guess you're a writer. Am I right?'

Kleinzeit half nodded, half shrugged.

'Poetry?'

'Little,' said Kleinzeit, 'now and then.'

'I'm very keen on poetry,' said Tede. 'I do Burns in Scots dialect.' He gave Kleinzeit a card:

ARTHUR TEDE

COMEDIAN – COMPERE – M.C.

POETRY RECITATIONS

(With Piano Accompaniment)

'My wife does the piano part,' said Tede. 'There's a lot in poetry, "more things in heaven and earth, Horatio, than are dreamt of in your philosophy," ha ha. During the day I'm an electrical engineer, but at night, you know, poetry.'

'Oh yes,' said Kleinzeit. He groaned tactfully to show that although interested he was probably enduring more pain than Tede dreamt of.

'You're looking thoughtful,' said Tede. '"*Il Penseroso*", the thoughtful one. Keep smiling is my motto. "*L'allegro*". Milton, you know. "Hence loathèd Melancholy, etcetera."'

Kleinzeit closed his eyes, nodded.

'Actually I'm doing that one now,' said Tede. 'Memorizing it. I keep adding to my repertoire. Do you mind following in the book while I try it aloud, see if I get it right. I've been wanting to do it for several days, but there's been no one I could ask till now, and one feels foolish reciting poetry alone.' He gave the book to Kleinzeit. Kleinzeit saw his hands holding it, didn't know how to let go. Tede was away:

178

'Hence loathèd Melancholy
Of Cerberus and blackest midnight born,
In Stygian Cave forlorn
'Mongst horrid shapes, and shreiks, and sights unholy, ...'

Kleinzeit fell asleep, woke up at 'Orpheus self'. 'What's
that?' he said.
'What's what?' said Tede. 'Have I got it wrong?'
'I've lost my place,' said Kleinzeit.
'Page 333, near the bottom,' said Tede.
Kleinzeit read:

Lap me in soft Lydian Aires,
Married to immortal verse
Such as the meeting soul may pierce
In notes, with many a winding bout
Of linckèd sweetnes long drawn out,
With wanton heed, and giddy cunning,
The melting voice through mazes running;
Untwisting all the chains that ty
The hidden soul of harmony.
That Orpheus self may heave his head
From golden slumber on a bed
Of heapt Elysian flowres, and hear
Such streins as would have won the ear
Of Pluto, to have quite set free
His half regain'd Eurydice.
These delights, if thou canst give,
Mirth with thee, I mean to live.

'Found it?' said Tede.
Kleinzeit nodded. Tede began again where he had left off,
Kleinzeit tried to shut out the voice so that he could hear
the words he was reading. Tede came to the end, his voice
stopped. Kleinzeit read the lines again, heard in his mind

the voice of the words alone going from the lapping of the soft Lydian Aires to:

> Untwisting all the chains that ty
> The hidden soul of harmony.

Inside him he felt a pause, as of an uplifted hand. Then it was as if a fat brush drew with black ink in one perfect sweep a circle, fat and black on yellow paper. Sweet, fresh, clear and simple. His whole organism was strong and sweetly rhythmic with the perfect health of it. Stay that way! he thought, felt it go as he thought it. Gone. Here he was again, sick, heavy, weak, full of 2-Nup, Zonk, Angle-Flex, Fly-Ova, and Lay-By. He began to cry.

'Moves you, doesn't it,' said Tede. 'Did you notice how I held "half regain'd" and sort of slid away on "Eurydice", then a pause to leave it in the air, then "These delights" etcetera; quiet but very up?'

'I have to be quiet for a while,' said Kleinzeit.

'Sorry,' said Tede. 'Didn't mean to overtax you.'

'What is harmony,' said Kleinzeit, 'but a fitting together.' He wasn't saying it to Tede but he had to say it aloud.

'That's an awfully good line,' said Tede. 'What's it from?'

'Nothing,' said Kleinzeit, and cried some more.

Everywhere, All the Time

Evening. Sister not on duty yet. Tede in the TV room. Kleinzeit listened to the words repeating themselves in his mind:

> Untwisting all the chains that ty
> The hidden soul of harmony.

It's hidden, right enough, said Kleinzeit.

You still here? said Hospital.

As soon as I can possibly go I will, I promise you, said Kleinzeit.

What're you waiting for, said Hospital. You've remembered yourself, haven't you.

I suppose I have done, said Kleinzeit. But it came and went so fast.

How long do you expect a moment to last, said Hospital.

But to have only one moment! said Kleinzeit.

Rubbish, said Hospital, and rang up Memory.

Memory here, said Memory.

Hall of Records, please, said Hospital.

Ringing for you now, said Memory. Here they are.

Hall of Records here, said Hall of Records.

The name is Kleinzeit, said Hospital. Could we have a few moments please. A random selection.

Moment, said Hall of Records: Spring, age something. Evening, the sky still light, the street lamps coming on. Harmony took place.

I remember, said Kleinzeit.

Moment, said Hall of Records: Summer, age something. Before a thunderstorm. Black sky. A piece of paper whirling in the air high over the street. Harmony took place.

I remember, said Kleinzeit. But so long ago!

Moment, said Hall of Records: Autumn, age something. Rain. The sound of the gas fire, Sister naked. Atlantis. Harmony took place.

Ah! said Kleinzeit.

Moment, said Hall of Records: Winter, age something. In hospital. Feeling of circle inside self, sweet rhythm. Harmony took place.

Kleinzeit waited.

Will there be anything else? said Hall of Records.

Place of dismemberment? said Kleinzeit.

Everywhere, all the time, said Hall of Records.

'Rather nicely stabilized, I should say,' said Dr Pink. 'I'm quite pleased with you actually.' Fleshky, Potluck and Krishna seemed pleased too.

Kleinzeit smiled modestly, wondered if that was a spot of blood on Fleshky's white coat. Probably some sort of chemical.

Dr Pink looked at the medication record on Kleinzeit's chart. 'Yes,' he said, 'I think we can take you off this lot.'

'Try something new, eh?' said Kleinzeit.

'No,' said Dr Pink. 'We'll just see how you do without any drugs, see how things go.' He's a devil, said the faces of the three young doctors. He'll try anything.

'You mean I'm all right now?' said Kleinzeit.

'That remains to be seen,' said Dr Pink, 'and I'm not making any promises. We'll see where we are in a few days.' He smiled, moved on with Fleshky, Potluck and Krishna.

Can you move over a little, said the bed. I can't seem to get comfortable.

Kleinzeit ignored it, huddled under the bedclothes. All at once the streets outside seemed one vast desolation, Underground the very abyss, the thought of sitting on that freezing floor with his glockenspiel was appalling. Fleets of Morton Taylor lorries thundered past, changing gears contemptuously. No window nearby, but unseen aeroplanes soared high in utter silence, bound for golden otherwheres.

'Good news, eh?' said Tede. 'That's why I always say Keep smiling.'

Kleinzeit made a gesture with two fingers on the side away from Tede, picked up some yellow paper, affected to be heavily absorbed in writing. What he wrote was:

Golden, Golden, Golden Virginia,
Be my tobacco, be my sin.

Not even original. Drogue's, that was. Was Drogue still
alive at the other end of the ward? Kleinzeit had been away
from there for a week now. They were all fading into the
past. What was there to say to Redbeard, Schwarzgang, and
the others, even if he got the nurse to wheel him to the old
neighbourhood.

The bed kept arching its back, trying to slide him off.
Hospital had had nothing to say for a long time. Word hadn't
dropped in either. The yellow paper was inert and lifeless
in his hands. Outside the hospital the winter sunlight walked
slowly past as if leaning on a cane. How had he come to this
with the yellow paper, like some dreadful marriage to a
frog princess who would always be a frog.

For a time there had been mystery, complexities, excite-
ment, riddles full of promise: the yellow-paper, foolscap,
and Rizla men, the permutations of barrow full of rocks, the
possibilites of STAFF ONLY and its key. None of it had been
explained, none of it mattered, he had no questions. He
reached under the bed. No one there. He thought of the
getaway with Pain Company. Those had been the days! He
yawned, fell asleep.

Walking like the winter sunlight but without a cane, Kleinzeit visited the other end of the ward. No drugs for five days now, and he felt simplified, economical, stripped-down and running on the cheapest possible fuel. His vision seemed plain and dull, lacking in colour. Everything looked smaller, sharper, shabbier. Astonishing how much paint was flaking off how many things. The chairs looked more second-hand than usual. The daylight in the ward seemed as if dispensed on a National Health prescription, slowly and with a numbered ticket, to the beds patiently queued up for it. The distant horn sounded as in the Beethoven overture, then a mild flash, A to B. Oh yes, said Kleinzeit. Everything is in good order now. We have laboured diligently and we are back where we started from.

Like Orpheus, said Hospital.

Yes indeed, said Kleinzeit. Orpheus on the National Health. A thrilling story, I'm surprised the B.B.C. haven't serialized it. Maybe Napalm Industries will film it. With Maximus Jock and Immensa Pudenda.

Your sarcasm is inappropriate, said Hospital.

So is everything else, said Kleinzeit, nodding hello as he passed one by one his sometime comrades. Nobody new gone. He sat down in the second-hand chair by Redbeard's second-hand bed. Redbeard looked like an abandoned car.

'Well,' said Kleinzeit.

'That's it,' said Redbeard. 'Well. You are and I'm not. The well can't talk to the sick.'

'But I'm not well,' said Kleinzeit. 'I feel the same as when I came to hospital.'

'That's more than most of us can say,' said Redbeard. You're one of the lucky ones.'

'I suppose I am.'

'And you'll be leaving.'

'I suppose I shall be.'

'There you are,' said Redbeard. 'Make the most of it.'

'I suppose I must,' said Kleinzeit. He walked slowly back to his bed, got there as Dr Pink arrived on his round with Fleshky, Potluck, and Krishna. All of them looked at him fondly, as an engine-driver might look at an engine that was being retired from service.

Pink examined him in a good-humoured way, clapped him on the shoulder when he had done. 'Well, old chap,' he said, 'that's it. We shan't keep you much longer. You can go home at the end of the week.'

Should I tell him, Kleinzeit wondered. 'That pain from A to B,' he said. 'It's back.'

'Oh yes,' said Dr Pink. 'That's to be expected, it's nothing out of the way really. You'll get that from time to time, but I shouldn't worry about it. That's just hypotenuse, you know, complaining a bit as we all do now and again.'

Well, that's that, thought Kleinzeit. I'm not going to ask any more questions, I don't want to know any more than I know now. 'Thank you for everything,' he said.

'All the best,' said Dr Pink. 'Come in and let me have a look at you in six months' time.'

'Thank you,' said Kleinzeit to Drs Fleshky, Potluck and Krishna. They all smiled broadly, seemed with their faces to say Thank *you*, like friendly waiters. But Kleinzeit felt as if he were the one who might be tipped.

Night. Kleinzeit asleep, Sister awake. The ward groaning, choking, sighing, snoring, splatting in bedpans. Sister in her lamplit binnacle, steadfastly pointing to her magnetic north. The sea rushing by on either side, the white bow wave gleaming in the dark.

Well, said God. Big day for you tomorrow, eh? Schwanzheit getting out.

Kleinzeit, said Sister. I don't think I want to talk about it, I don't want to do anything unlucky.

Not to worry, said God. You'll have luck. You're lucky.

Do you mean that, said Sister. Am I really? It hasn't always seemed that way to me.

Well of course it never does, said God. I don't say you're *especially* lucky. Just a good ordinary everyday sort of luck. That's as much as I've got myself, and I don't know anyone who's got more. Universe, History, Eternity, anybody you talk to these days, we're all in the same boat.

I wouldn't know, said Sister. I don't ever talk to them. I don't think very big.

And you're quite right not to, said God. Just carry on as you are, and all the best to both of you. I really mean that.

Thank you, said Sister.

You're moving into his flat? said God.

I expect so, said Sister.

What's he got there, gas or electricity?

It's all electric.

I'll see if I can put off the electrical strike for a week or so, said God. Give you a chance to start off with cooker, fridge and heating all in working order. Sort of a wedding present.

That's really very kind of you, said Sister. I appreciate that.

Well, said God, I'm off then. We'll stay in touch.

Oh yes, said Sister. Thanks so much.

Not a bad sort, God, said Hospital. In His own fumbling way.

He's a lot nicer than you are, said Sister.

I'm not so bad, said Hospital. I talk rough, maybe, but I'm a decent chap.

Hmmph, said Sister.

What I said about Kleinzeit not getting to keep you, said Hospital, Eurydice and all that, I didn't mean it the way you thought. I just meant ultimately, you know, in the long run. He can have you for as long as he lasts.

Or as long as I last, said Sister. Or as long as it lasts. I'm not looking ahead.

However you like to put it, said Hospital, I shan't interfere. I just wait about while things take their course. I'd like to give you a little present too.

That *is* nice of you, said Sister. I wasn't expecting anything like that.

It's nothing much, said Hospital. The odds were on Kleinzeit to come down with the flu next week but I steered it in another direction. I think it's heading for Dr Bashan. Of course Kleinzeit'll probably get it the week after. I can't really change anything.

But an extra week without it is lovely, said Sister. Thanks so much.

Ahem, said Word. We haven't met.

No, said Sister. I don't recognize your voice.

No matter, said Word. I've a present for you too.

It's lovely, getting all these presents, said Sister.

Wherever there's a barrow full of rocks, said Word,
you'll be there too.

Is that a present? said Sister.

Yes indeed, said Word.

Thank you, said Sister. You've all been so kind.

Middle of the night. Sister in the bedroom asleep, taking a fortnight's holiday from the hospital. Kleinzeit awake at the plain deal table in the bare sitting-room. Sister's clock ticking on the wall, Sister's Turkoman cushions heaped in a corner with her velvet elephant, woollen rabbit, shining helmet. Candle burning in a saucer on the plain deal table. Yellow paper pages piling up.

Hoo hoo, a hoarse whisper at the door. Anybody awake?

Is this a professional call or a social one? said Kleinzeit.

Social, said Death. I just happen to be in the neighbourhood, thought I'd look in.

Kleinzeit opened the door, they went into the sitting-room. Kleinzeit sat in the chair, Death sat on the cushions in the corner. They nodded at each other, smiled, shrugged.

Care for a banana? said Kleinzeit.

Thanks, said Death. I don't eat bananas. How's it going?

Can't complain, said Kleinzeit. Couple of pages a day. Tomorrow I'll start busking again.

You're doing all right, said Death. I've a present for you.

What? said Kleinzeit. No tricks, I hope.

No tricks, said Death.

Where is it? said Kleinzeit. I don't see anything.

Tell you later, said Death.

Kleinzeit lit a cigarette, sat smoking by candlelight. There's something I've wanted to do, he said. I don't know if I can.

What? said Death.

Kleinzeit took a bottle of black ink and a fat Japanese brush out of the plain deal table drawer. He took a piece of yellow paper, dipped the brush in the ink, poised it over the paper.

You can do it, said Death.

Kleinzeit touched the paper with the brush, drew in one smooth sweep a fat black circle, sweet and round.

That's it, said Death. My present.

Thank you, said Kleinzeit. He tacked the yellow paper to the wall near the clock. Let's go for a walk, he said.

They went down to the river. The lights on the embankment were dark, but the street lights were still on. Night almost gone, the bridges black against a sky growing pale. Cold, the air, and wet. The river running lapping at the wall, ebbing to the sea. No moon to light the head of Orpheus wherever it was swimming. Death swung along at Kleinzeit's side, its black back bobbing up and down. Neither said anything.

I'll turn off here, said Death when they came to the third bridge. See you.

See you, said Kleinzeit. He watched Death's small black going-away shape rising and falling as it swung off out of sight under the street lamps.